THE HORSEMAN

MARCIA LYNN McCLURE

Published by Distractions Ink
1290 Mirador Loop N.E.
Rio Rancho, NM 87144

Published by Distractions Ink
©Copyright 2015 by M. Meyers
A.K.A. Marcia Lynn McClure
Cover Photography by ©George Kroll/Dreamstime.com
and ©Sofiaworld/Dreamstime.com
Cover Design and Interior Graphics by Sandy Ann Allred/Timeless Allure

First Printed Edition: October 2015
All character names and personalities in this work of fiction are entirely
fictional, created solely in the imagination of the author.
Any resemblance to any person living or dead is coincidental.

McClure, Marcia Lynn, 1965—
The Horseman: a novel/by Marcia Lynn McClure.

ISBN: 978-0-9861307-8-6
Library of Congress Control Number: 2015953538
Printed in the United States of America

__To Gina—__
For being a solace and healer to my soul,
An inspiration and beacon of respite for my mind,
And (unknowingly) reminding me last week
that I need to write something beautiful every day!

CHAPTER ONE

Mrs. Enola Fletcher had been a reasonable woman. Certainly she'd been a woman who believed that her great wealth and family name entitled her to immediate respect and that a good measure of servitude should be provided her, by each and every human being on earth. Still, her tongue was not too sharp, and she did smile and laugh a bit here and there. Indeed, Enola Fletcher had owned moments of humility (albeit very few) and greater kindness than some sharing her high rank of social stature.

Therefore, as Briney stood watching the train pull away from the small station platform, studying the large boxcar in which Mrs. Fletcher's casket rested, she felt new tears of compassion and mourning brimming in her eyes. A man closed the boxcar door just as the train's caboose rattled past, and then she was gone. Mrs. Fletcher was gone.

Exhaling a heavy sigh of blended sorrow, trepidation, and even guilty reprieve, Briney turned and descended the plank stairs of the train platform. The past few days had seemed like a bad dream—as if they couldn't have truly heaped upon Briney what they had. In fact,

Briney was so entirely awash with the sensation of surrealism that she paused before heading back to the boardinghouse in town—paused to glance about at her surroundings, breathe in a deep breath of fresh, free air, and assure herself that she really was standing near the train station in little-known Oakmont, Colorado, having just sent her dead benefactress's earthly remains on their journey east to New York. Mrs. Fletcher's children would see to her burial there. After a few more moments of reflection, Briney was convinced that Mrs. Enola Fletcher really was gone and that, for the first time in near to ten years, Briney Thress was on her own.

Straightening her posture, Briney started down the dusty main road leading to Oakmont. At first, she quickened her step. After all, it was her habit to walk quickly any time Mrs. Fletcher wasn't with her—in that Mrs. Fletcher could hardly do without Briney for one moment and therefore forever and always told her to, "Hurry, Briney! Hasten your step, for I do not want to be long without your company."

But even as the memory of Mrs. Fletcher's demands that Briney "hurry" pricked at her mind, Briney slowed her pace to that of a body having nowhere to be at no particular time. After all, Briney had no pressing reason to hurry—no elderly woman waiting impatiently at home for her, expecting to be entertained in some fashion.

Yet Briney found such a slow pace was far *too* slow. She was not at all used to strolling and thus sped her step a bit—to a pace she rather guessed might resemble that of ambling.

"Yes," Briney whispered to herself as her face at last donned a smile. "I mean to amble back to town…walk at my leisure."

It was another thing Briney hadn't been able to do for almost half of her life—speak her thoughts aloud—and she found it invigorating!

Suddenly, however, her thoughts began to flood her mind in an overwhelming cascade of worrisome succession. She wondered whether she would truly be able to provide for herself the necessities of life, even *with* the generous sum of money Mrs. Fletcher had gifted Briney hours before her passing—for she truly had no idea how to figure what her needs would cost her in the years to come. Likewise, she began to worry that perhaps the Kelleys hadn't truly meant what they'd said—that Briney could stay at their boardinghouse for as long as she needed or wanted to. Perhaps they had simply felt sorry for Briney when Mrs. Fletcher (Briney's sole financial support and semblance of family) had passed away so unexpectedly, leaving her charge, for all intents and purposes, homeless. Perhaps pity was the only reason the proprietors of the Oakmont boardinghouse had offered her a permanent room in their establishment.

Other worries raced through Briney's mind as she walked. She'd always felt lonesome—her entire life. But at least she'd had Mrs. Fletcher to talk to! Whom would she converse with now? Whom would she serve? What would she do with her time?

With anxiety fast filling her bosom near to bursting, Briney's attempt at ambling was all too soon replaced by her usual hurrying pace.

For one thing, Briney knew she'd feel better about everything once she'd returned to the boardinghouse. Not only was the money Mrs. Fletcher had gifted her hidden in her room—along with all her worldly possessions—but Bethanne Kelley would be at hand, as well. Bethanne had been such a comfort to Briney over the past few days. Truth be told, even before poor Mrs. Fletcher had passed, Bethanne had quickly earned Briney's gratitude and affection, and Briney knew that just the simplest of conversations with Bethanne would lighten her own anxious mood.

Bethanne Kelley was the daughter of Walter and Sylvia Kelley, the proprietors of the Oakmont boardinghouse. And it had been Bethanne who had first greeted and welcomed Mrs. Fletcher and Briney to Oakmont. Briney would never forget the moment she first met Bethanne, for she was so astonished at the girl's radiant countenance and pleasant, easy manner of conversation that she'd immediately thought her the brightest, kindest person she'd ever in all her life met.

Bethanne was taller than Briney, with beautiful strawberry-blonde hair—the color of hair Briney had always wished she'd been born with, instead of her own rather "snuff-colored" hair, as Mrs. Fletcher had once termed the shade. And Bethanne had beautiful blue eyes— eyes the color of the late summer sky. Briney knew her own eyes, though blue, were nothing as bright and inviting as Bethanne's were.

"Your eyes remind me of two pieces of cobalt sea glass I once found while beachcombing in the southern states—dark and cold," had once been how Mrs. Fletcher described Briney's eyes.

Still, Briney wasn't envious of Bethanne and her rare beauty of spirit and face—only admiring of her. Not only was Bethanne radiantly pretty, but she also owned a heart of gold and a manner of sincere kindness that Briney had rarely experienced.

Bethanne was entertaining as well. Oh, not in the way Briney had to be entertaining when caring for Mrs. Fletcher. It wasn't Bethanne's ability to read aloud to another person for hours on end or to sit and listen to Mrs. Fletcher ramble on and on and on for more hours on end that made Bethanne entertaining. It was her wit and remarkable sense of humor, her ability to see everything in life as either lovely or amusing. Briney admired that quality in Bethanne most of all and often wondered if she herself might have been a more jovial sort had her life circumstances been different.

Therefore, the moment Briney stepped back into the boardinghouse after having sent Mrs. Fletcher's earthly remains on to New York by way of the train, she instantly felt more hopeful—relieved and less anxious.

Exhaling a heavy sigh of compassion, Bethanne placed a hand on Briney's shoulder, smiled with sympathy, and asked, "I suppose it's done then? Is dear Mrs. Fletcher on her way to New York?"

Briney nodded, comforted by Bethanne's concern. "Yes," she answered, nodding.

"So the old girl is off to New York, and you're a free woman now, eh, Briney?" Mr. Kelley asked, striding through the entryway toward the parlor. His arms were filled with wood, no doubt intended to restock the wood basket near the parlor hearth.

"Daddy!" Bethanne scolded. "Don't be so indelicate!" Bethanne placed a reassuring arm around Briney's shoulders. "Why, Briney's just lost someone very near and dear to her. I'm sure her heart is still very tender."

"I'm sure it is," Mr. Kelley called from the parlor. "But I seen the way that old bat treated you, Briney," he added, striding into the entryway once more. "And I don't mean to sound hardhearted, but I feel like your bonds of slavery have been loosed, and now you can make your own life…and in whatever way you see fit."

Briney couldn't help but smile at Mr. Kelley's forthright explanation of things. Part of her did mourn Mrs. Fletcher's passing. Yet if she were to confess the truth to anyone, she felt exactly as Mr. Kelley said—as if her bonds of slavery had been loosed and she'd been set free.

"I-I know it might sound just morbid," Briney began, glancing away uncomfortably for a moment, "but I do feel a mingling of fear and trepidation, loneliness…yet freedom and excitement that I've not felt in so, so long."

Bethanne took Briney's hands in her own. Staring into her face and nodding, Bethanne encouraged, "Go on. It's all right to say it, Briney. Truly it is."

It was as if some pent-up emotion Briney had never allowed herself to express burst from her bosom, up through her throat, and out of her mouth before she could attempt to stop it.

"I had everything I ever needed—food, shelter, clothing," she began. "Nice clothing, comfortable shelter, and the majority of the time better food than most people enjoy on a regular basis. As far as temporal needs, I wanted for nothing."

"Perhaps not," Bethanne said. "But…but it doesn't seem as if you had much…well, much fun, much merriment at all."

Briney nodded and continued. "No…no, not much. But I was far happier and better cared for than I would've been had I been forced to stay in the orphanage until I was eighteen. And even then, what future awaited me when I was of age and turned out from the institution?" She sighed, burying her disappointment in having lived a life of servitude in Mrs. Fletcher's care in favor of being content with the fact she had not had to linger cold, alone, starving, beaten, and neglected in the orphanage asylum. "In truth, it was a life many young ladies would diligently seek after, I suppose. As Mrs. Fletcher's companion, I've been to nearly every country in Europe. I've seen lions and elephants on the vast plains of Africa, lingered in grand palaces in South America."

"It *does* sound adventurous," Bethanne commented. "I suppose an exciting life the likes you have lived would be preferable to the simple days and nights we all of us linger in here."

It was then that Briney could no longer bury her disappointment at having been so lonesome for so long. As tears welled in her eyes, she looked to Bethanne, placed a firm hand on her friend's arm, and said, "No, the path that brought me here was not a joyous one, Bethanne. It was lonely, solitary in so many ways, and entirely void of any mirth and laughter that was my own. I would not wish it on anyone, other than those who have had to endure the worse existence of life in an orphanage or asylum. You have had a wonderful, beautiful life, filled with family, love, and joy. No sort of luxurious travel, no lingering in the shadow of the Taj Mahal or any other edifice of history, can compare to a simple life bursting with friends, family, and even hard work. Always remember that. Your upbringing was a blessing…and the stuff of my dreams."

Briney heard Mr. Kelley clear his throat. She and Bethanne glanced at him quickly, only to look back to one another with grins of mild amusement at the fact they'd seen him dabbing tears from his eyes with the sleeve of his shirt.

"Well, I best get back to my business," Mr. Kelley mumbled. "But I will say that we're mighty glad you landed here with us, Briney Thress. Mighty glad. We might not be the Taj Mahal, but we've got good food, comfortable rooms, and a hell of a lot more character than the old bat who brought you here and then up and died on ya. I hope you'll stay on as long as you like with us."

Briney smiled. "Thank you, Mr. Kelley," she told him. "And I hope you mean that, because I don't plan on leaving any time soon."

"Oh, I'm so glad to hear you say that, Briney!" Bethanne squealed, throwing her arms around her friend. "I was afraid you might not like our simple way of life, that you might decide you still wanted to travel."

Returning Bethanne's warm embrace, Briney sighed. "Not at all," she assured her friend. "I would be perfectly content to never have to board another ship or even a train for that matter…not ever again!"

"I gotta go slop the hogs," Mr. Kelley mumbled, again wiping the moisture of emotion from his eyes with his shirtsleeve.

He strode away then, and when he was gone, Bethanne giggled, whispering, "Daddy's a tenderhearted soul, no matter how hard he tries to convince us otherwise. He didn't mean to sound so…so…callous about poor Mrs. Fletcher's passin'."

Briney nodded her reassurance to Bethanne that she wasn't at all offended. "Oh, I know that." She shrugged, adding, "And besides, he's correct in his observations."

Bethanne breathed a sigh of relief in knowing her father hadn't offended Briney.

"Well, I think you've had enough chaos and worry these past few days to last a body a lifetime," Bethanne began. "So why don't you run on up to your room and rest a while? Read a book or…or just take a little nap or somethin'. I'll come and get you for supper."

"Oh, I couldn't possibly just…just do nothing at all," Briney argued, however. She felt abruptly nervous and unsettled. She wasn't at all used to having time to herself.

"Of course you can!" Bethanne exclaimed. "Why, you've done nothing but send telegrams, prepare Mrs. Fletcher's belongin's, mourn, and worry these past three days. You need some rest." Bethanne grinned mischievously, lowered her voice to a whisper, and added, "I left a couple of my favorite dime novels up in your room for ya. Although I'm sure Mrs. Fletcher would not have approved of you readin' the likes of stories about cowboys and outlaws."

Briney's smile broadened. "All the more reason to read them then," she giggled in a whisper.

Bethanne laughed. "Then it's settled! You run on up and rest or read or whatever you have a mind to do. I'll see you at supper, all right?"

"All right," Briney agreed. All at once she'd realized just how tired she really was. It had indeed been three very long, very taxing, very emotional days, and she imagined a bit of respite and time to think without Mrs. Fletcher and her passing to worry about would be very restful.

"And by the way, Briney," Bethanne called after her, "a black ribbon is plenty good enough for mournin' after your Mrs. Fletcher, at least out here in our neck of the woods. Why don't you wear somethin' bright and happy when you come down for supper?"

Briney paused in ascending the stairs and looked back to Bethanne in astonishment. "Oh, surely you can't be in earnest, Bethanne!" she exclaimed. "Why, I'm sure I'm meant to wear all black crape for at least six months! I can't just—"

"You certainly can, Briney," Bethanne said, placing her hands on her hips to emphasize her firmness of opinion. "Out here, folks don't stand so hard on black crape for mourning, even for widows. Why, the longest I've ever seen a widow in black here in Oakmont was when ol' Mrs. Ada Rose Josephson lost her husband, Mr. Josiah Josephson. Mrs. Josephson wore black crape and a veil for all of two months and then nearly passed out from the heat one day while walkin' through town. She took to wearing just a black hat after that." Bethanne shook her head. "You're a bright young woman, Briney, and your life is your own now. No one 'round here will give a second thought to you not bein' shrouded in black like the grim reaper." Bethanne folded her arms across her chest, adding, "And besides, Mrs. Fletcher…she wasn't even your kin in truth now, was she?"

Briney couldn't help but smile at Bethanne. She was standing at the foot of the stairs looking so determined that she quite convinced Briney.

"Well, things out here do seem to differ very broadly from back east," Briney admitted.

"Yep! And that's how we like it," Bethanne confirmed. "So no black crape at supper, okay? It'll ruin everybody's meal anyhow."

Briney allowed a quiet giggle to escape her throat—a giggle Mrs. Fletcher would have entirely disapproved of.

"Very well. No more black crape," Briney agreed.

Bethanne nodded with approval.

Briney was still smiling when she reached her small but comfortable room. Bethanne Kelley was a very strong-minded young woman—a confident young woman who seemed never to doubt herself, her abilities, or her decisions. Briney hoped to one day have the strength of character and self-belief Bethanne had.

Briney exhaled a heavy sigh as she stripped off the uncomfortable black crape dress she'd been wearing for the past three days. It was the most uncomfortable dress she owned, and she was glad to free her body of its dismal black. Though she knew she would struggle in changing her ways from the proper, polite practice of perfect etiquette demanded by Mrs. Fletcher, Briney was inwardly exuberant at the anticipation of a more informal way of life the likes lived in small western towns like Oakmont.

She'd thought she'd be wearing the gloomy black crape for six months, in the least. And the sudden knowledge that she could cast it aside and wear whatever she chose lifted her spirits to a height she'd not known since she was a child.

Briney rather plopped down on her comfortable bed, closing her eyes as the breeze from the open window next to it breathed over her. The lace of the curtains tickled her nose as they wafted to and fro as the fragrant breeze manipulated them, and she giggled, thinking how utterly mortified Mrs. Fletcher would be to know that Briney was lying on her bed in nothing but her undergarments—and doing nothing at all.

Still, her respite was short-lived, for there was one task that needed tending before Briney could relax altogether. The money must be hidden!

Oh, it wasn't that Briney hadn't already hidden the money. She'd hidden it the moment Mrs. Fletcher had given it to her, only hours before the poor old woman had passed. But with all the preparations Briney had found herself making in order to have Mrs. Fletcher's earthly remains transported back to New York to her family, Briney hadn't really had the time to consider a truly safe hiding place for the money.

Sitting upright on her bed, Briney went to the traveling trunk at the foot of it—the trunk that kept safe all of her sentimental possessions and a few necessities as well. Opening the trunk, Briney carefully removed items, setting them aside, until she uncovered the two old biscuit tins Mrs. Fletcher had presented to her.

As Briney removed the tins from the trunk, she was once more struck by the weight of them. Yet what had she expected? One thousand silver dollars should be heavy! Setting aside the biscuit tins full of coins, Briney removed a tobacco tin from inside the trunk. This was the tin that Briney worried most about losing—the tobacco tin filled with $1,500 worth of banknotes of various denominations. To Briney, the silver coins in the biscuit tins simply seemed more durable than the paper money in the tobacco tin. Regardless of which form of the money was to be worried over the most, she knew that both the coins and the banknotes needed to be hidden, for it was all she had in the world with which to provide for herself the necessities of life.

As Briney glanced around her room, she knew that it would be wise to divide the money and hide it in several different locations, rather than hiding it all together for one burglar to stumble across. But she was tired from the demands of the past few days and therefore chose a hiding place nearby that would serve better than the obvious trunk of valuables.

She began in the wardrobe, searching the back paneling for any loose boards that might prove a secure place to keep at least some of the money. When the wardrobe proved to be no help, Briney investigated the chest of drawers but decided a drawer would be as obvious a place as a trunk to look if one were robbing someone.

At last, Briney determined there was no good place to hide Mrs. Fletcher's gift—not in her boardinghouse room anyway. She would need to find another place to keep it, perhaps out away from town somewhere—maybe buried under a tree or bush. But in order to cache the money away from town, Briney knew she would need some sort of conveyance or at least a horse.

Pure exhilaration welled in Briney at once then, and she whispered, "A horse! A horse of my very own!"

Opening the tobacco tin, she gazed at the banknotes with in. A twenty-dollar note lay on top of the pile of notes. "I'll buy my own horse!" she giggled to herself.

Oh, all her life Briney had dreamt of owning a horse—a horse she could ride at her leisure, ride whenever and wherever she wanted to go. And now, as she stood in her lovely little boardinghouse room, staring down at the wealth of money in the tobacco tin, she knew that she had the ability to make her dream come true for herself.

"Yes!" she said, still smiling as she tucked the two biscuit tins and one tobacco tin back into the deepest part of her trunk. "Tomorrow I'll buy a horse! And I'll ride it out to wherever I want!"

Plopping down on her bed once more, she sighed. "And I'll ride my horse astride instead of sidesaddle. For I'm a woman of the west now, and I mean to avoid black dresses, ride astride on my magnificent horse, and feel the wind in my hair and the sun on my face completely careless of whether or not I turn freckled for it!"

And then, for the first time in a decade—as the late summer breeze blew the lace curtains of the window out over her bed and body to soothe and lull her—Briney Thress fell asleep in the very middle of the day, without one concern of whether she would be scolded for it.

"In my day, mourning was simply miserable!" Mrs. Abbot said. "A widow was required to wear black crape head to toe for the entire first year. I remember my poor mother being so miserable in that crape after Daddy passed. It wasn't bad enough that she was left alone with us eight children and a broken heart; society demanded that she be in physical misery as well." Mrs. Abbot shook her white-haired head, adding, "I'm glad things out west here are different where mourning rituals are concerned."

"I certainly concur," Mr. Davenport agreed. "Women had the worst of it, of course. And it seemed like every woman and child in every town was draped in black during the war. And I don't think that did one bit of good toward raising folks' spirits none then either."

"Goodness no," Mrs. Abbot replied.

He nodded his own white-haired head at Mrs. Abbot and smiled at her. Briney knew, by the look of understanding that passed between the two eldest boarders at the boardinghouse, that they had both lived war-torn lives and thus had a knowledge of how truly painful life could be—a knowledge the others at the table did not own.

"Well, I think that even though Mrs. Fletcher, God rest her soul, was your guardian, Miss Thress…I think a black ribbon round your arm there is plenty of mourning garb for a young girl like you," Mrs. Kelley offered. "She wasn't a blood relative, after all…God rest her soul."

"See?" Bethanne said, smiling at Briney. "I told you no one would think anything at all of your not wearing full mourning dress. Things are different in Oakmont."

Briney nodded, feeling more relieved than ever. She didn't want to show any disrespect toward Mrs. Fletcher, but neither did she want to dress all in stiff, itchy black crape for a woman who had treated her more like a slave than a ward.

"And now that that's settled," Mr. Kelley began, "have you had any ideas of what you'd like to do with your life now, Briney?"

"Walt, don't press the girl!" Mrs. Kelley quietly scolded her husband. "For Pete's sake! She's only just put the woman on a train this very day."

Smiling, however, Briney ventured, "Well, I have decided to stay on here in Oakmont…at least for a time."

"Oh, joy!" Mrs. Abbot explained.

Bethanne giggled. "Thank goodness!"

"I think that's a right fine decision," Mr. Kelley interjected. "Oakmont has a lot to offer."

"I hope you'll stay on with us here at the boardinghouse as long as you want, Briney," Mrs. Kelley offered. "You know we'd love to keep you forever, if things work out that way."

Briney smiled, feeling truly welcomed and wanted. "I do want to stay on at the boardinghouse," she admitted. Then, inhaling a deep breath, she added, "And I think I'd like to purchase a horse—my own horse—so I can ride out whenever I want to. I've always wanted to ride."

"Oh, that's a fine idea!" Mr. Davenport exclaimed. "There ain't nothing in all the world as liberating as riding out away from civilization and just being alone with your own thoughts."

"I love to ride," Bethanne said. "Have you ever ridden a horse, Briney?"

Briney nodded as she swallowed a bite of her mashed potatoes. "Oh yes. Mrs. Fletcher made sure I was well trained…although I was never allowed to ride astride as the women out here do. Always only sidesaddle."

"Well, riding astride is much more comfortable…at least in my opinion," Mrs. Abbot commented. "I too was taught to ride sidesaddle, but after my late husband and I moved out here, I never rode sidesaddle again."

"I've always ridden astride," Bethanne explained. "And I have an extra riding skirt if you'd like to borrow it until we can get one made up for you, Briney."

"You mean, the split skirt kind…like trousers, only…" Briney began to ask.

"Exactly!" Bethanne confirmed. "I'm sure you've seen ladies around town wearing them. They're all the rage out here where we girls ride astride instead of sidesaddle."

"You need to go on out to the Horseman's place," Mr. Davenport suggested.

"Oh, absolutely," Mr. Kelley emphatically agreed. "Cole's the best horseman in six counties…at least! He'll find you a mount that's perfect for you and what you want, Briney."

"Cole?" Briney asked.

"Mr. Cole, the Horseman," Mrs. Kelley explained. "He owns a ranch just three miles west of town, and he's got so many horses, they're practically comin' out of his ears!"

"I agree," Mr. Davenport said. "Just skip the livery altogether and let Cole set you up with a horse. He'll do it for a good price too…and probably board it for you."

Excitement welled inside Briney's bosom. A horse! Her very own horse! The thought made her happier than she'd felt in a very long time. She could just imagine the freedom owning her own horse would afford her, and she decided then and there she'd venture out to the ranch outside of town the very next morning and talk to this "horseman" about a horse.

"I'll pay the Horseman a visit then, first thing in the morning," Briney said, smiling. "Then maybe by the time I sit down to supper with you all tomorrow evening, I'll be the owner of my very own horse."

Everyone laughed and offered verbal encouragements. Briney could hardly wait for supper to be over so that she could get to bed. That way morning would be just a night's sleep away, and she would wake to the possibility of owning her own horse.

Briney Thress had hardly owned anything at all, in all her life, let alone something as wonderful and valuable as a horse. Oh, certainly she had the fine dresses and even some jewelry Mrs. Fletcher had purchased for her over the years. But those were more for Mrs.

Fletcher's benefit than Briney's. Mrs. Fletcher had explained—on the very day she'd come to the orphanage, chosen Briney to be her traveling companion, and taken her away—that Briney must always be dressed in a manner that reflected well upon Mrs. Fletcher. And so it was Briney had always been dressed, if not lavishly at times, at least very well to do. Therefore, until Mrs. Fletcher had passed away, Briney had never even considered the clothes she wore her own. They always only seemed borrowed somehow.

Thus the very idea—the hope—of owning a horse caused boundless elation to well within Briney.

And so after supper and after a friendly visit with everyone in the parlor, Briney took her leave of the owners and other boarders and hurried upstairs to her comfortable room.

As she readied for bed, Briney was so excited at the prospect of what might transpire the next day that she wondered how in all the world she would manage to settle down and get to sleep.

"A horse of my own? I can hardly imagine it!" Briney whispered to herself as she changed her day dress for a nightgown.

As she climbed into bed and blew out the flame of the oil lamp on the night table next to it, she whispered, "Will it be a bay? Perhaps a chestnut or buckskin?"

Although Briney had never owned her own horse, she had read about them at great length whenever she was afforded the loan of a book of equine subject and therefore knew somewhat about equine breeds, colors, and identifying marks.

Exhaling a heavy sigh, Briney turned over in her bed, closed her eyes, and tried not to think of horses—tried not to imagine herself riding astride a beautiful horse all her own—tried not to wonder what it would feel like to let the sun freckle her face.

Almost instantly, however, Briney's eyes popped open.

"I'll never get to sleep!" she moaned.

And then—then she wondered. As the clock resting atop the chest of drawers chimed the half hour, Briney strained her ears in listening—in hoping.

Several days before Mrs. Fletcher's passing, Mr. and Mrs. Kelley had offered Briney her very own room at the boardinghouse. Briney and Mrs. Fletcher had been sharing a room, of course, being that Mrs. Fletcher always wanted Briney at hand. Yet when Mrs. Fletcher's illness had begun to worsen so hastily, the kind proprietors of the boardinghouse had recognized Briney's discomfort and inability to sleep for the sake of poor Mrs. Fletcher's being in the same room. Therefore, they'd offered her her own room. And when Mrs. Fletcher had passed on to the next life, Briney had asked if she could stay in the room the Kelleys had offered her, paying board until she was sure of what she should do next.

And it had been that first night in her own room when Briney had heard his voice. While lying in her bed and feeling a bit guilty in enjoying being alone, through the open window Briney had heard a group of men begin a discussion.

The air had been just right to carry the voices of the men up from the hitching post in front of the little restaurant Mr. and Mrs. Kelley operated (located just beneath Briney's room) and in through Briney's open bedroom window.

The men had begun a friendly conversation over the weather. And although the sounds of all the men's voices intrigued Briney, it was one voice in particular that had served to truly mesmerize her! This voice, belonging to a man the others referred to as Gunner, was as smooth and rich as molasses. Deep but not too deep, the man called Gunner's voice served to somehow lull Briney—settle her ragged nerves and chase away her anxieties.

Since that first night near to a week before, Briney had lain in bed each night waiting for the men to leave the restaurant and pause at the hitching post to converse. Sadly, the men didn't eat at the restaurant every night, but for four of the seven nights Briney had been in her own room, they had—and she hoped tonight would be another night that found the men, especially Gunner, pausing at the hitching post to talk.

Briney's heart leapt in her bosom as in the very next moment, she heard one man say, "Hey there, Gunner. You headed back to the ranch then?"

"I sure am," the voice belonging to Gunner answered. "My back's achin' like I've been sleepin' on a board for a month."

"Oh, I hear that," the other voice chuckled. "I had me a heifer wander off this mornin', and I spent half the day huntin' her down. Didn't get much else done, so now I'm behind all the more than I was when I woke up this mornin'."

"Oh, I hear ya there, Ethan," Gunner's soothing voice chuckled. "And now it feels like the wind is about to come up, and I got chores to do back home before I can hit the hay."

"I sure don't care much for the wind," the man named Ethan commented.

"Me neither," Gunner said. "The way it gets to howlin' and moanin' out at my place…it sounds like an old dog tryin' to outrun death, and it keeps me up at night. Know what I mean?"

"Oh, I do, Gunner, I surely do," Ethan said. "Well, you have a good evenin' all the same now."

"You too, Ethan."

Briney closed her eyes, smiling. A cool breeze, fragrant with the scent of flowers and herbs drifting on the air from somewhere, billowed the curtains at the window out over her bed. She didn't even realize she'd fallen asleep until she awoke the next morning with the bright light of day lighting up the room—having dreamt all the night long of riding her very own horse as the invigorating sense of the wind in her hair and the warm sun on her face cheered her.

CHAPTER TWO

"Cole's place is about three miles down the main road goin' outta town this way," Mr. Kelley said, pointing west as he stood with Briney on the front porch of the boardinghouse the next morning. "You just keep walkin' west, and you can't miss it."

"Are you sure you don't want one of my ridin' skirts, Briney?" Bethanne asked.

"Oh no, not today," Briney assured her. "I don't want Mr. Cole to think I'm so assuming as all that...just walking up to his property and expecting to ride a horse at once."

"But what if you do decide to ride?" Bethanne asked.

"Oh, I'm sure it won't be as easy as all that, Bethanne," Briney answered. "After all, I don't have a saddle or anything." Keenly aware of her own disappointment in the knowledge that it may be days and days before she would actually be able to ride her horse—if indeed Mr. Cole, the Horseman, even had a horse for sale—Briney forced a smile and added, "I'm sure I'll need a split skirt soon enough. But today I'll probably just be talking with the man about purchasing a horse."

"Well, if you're sure," Bethanne sighed with obvious disappointment. She brightened almost immediately, however. "It is a lovely walk, no matter what the outcome today, Briney. Enjoy yourself, all right?"

"I will," Briney promised her friend. Frowning with concern then, she turned to Mr. Kelley and asked, "And you're certain it's appropriate for me just to walk on out there by myself... unescorted?"

Mr. Kelley chuckled. "Aw, hell yes, Briney! Folks out here don't have time to stand on too much ceremony with things like that. You need a horse, and Cole is the man who will have one to sell ya. So you just trot on out there and let him know what you need." Mr. Kelley paused, and Briney fancied he blushed a little. "But I'd be glad to come with you if you like."

"That's very kind of you, Mr. Kelley," Briney said, delighted by the uncharacteristic shyness in his countenance at that moment. "But I know you and Mrs. Kelley have a lot to do before the restaurant opens for lunch today. I'll be fine, thank you."

"All-righty then," Mr. Kelley said, looking somewhat relieved. "Then you just follow the road out about three miles, and when you see a big red barn loomin' on the horizon...well, that's Cole's place."

Inhaling a breath of courage and determination, Briney nodded. "Well, I'm on my way then. Wish me luck!" she said.

Bethanne offered a quick embrace of reassurance and said, "You'll be fine! It'll be an adventure—one you've never had before, right?"

"Exactly!" Briney agreed. "I've never purchased anything for myself in all my life, let alone walked three miles all by myself."

"Good luck," Bethanne said.

"Thank you," Briney giggled a little nervously. "I'll be fine."

"Yes, you will," Bethanne encouraged.

Stepping down from the boardinghouse porch, onto the town boardwalk, and then onto Oakmont's dusty main road, Briney began walking west. She was unsettled a bit by the way her hands were trembling—by the way she still half-expected Mrs. Fletcher to call out in scolding her for running off on her own.

In fact, as her trembling continued—even as she walked past the general store and the livery, the last buildings on the west end of town—Briney wondered if she'd ever get over the constant feeling that she was about to be scolded for doing something she wanted to do—for thinking her own mind. Yet it was something she certainly *must* get over if she expected to truly enjoy living her own life. Mrs. Fletcher was gone—dead, to think of it bluntly. The elderly woman would never be scolding Briney at every turn ever again, and Briney knew she must train herself to be confident, be wise, make her own decisions, and set free aspects of her character and personality that she'd had to keep hidden for the past ten years.

Just outside of town, several pretty finches startled from a tree as Briney passed. Smiling as a peculiar sense of delighted anticipation rose in her bosom at watching them flitter about, Briney quickened her step in the direction Mr. Kelley had indicated. Three miles wasn't so far, and it had been a long time since Briney had been able to meander at her own pace anywhere at all—let alone along such a beautiful, rural setting. Very quickly, she found the town was already far enough behind her that the only sounds she could discern were the lulling warbles of songbirds and the soothing breeze through the leaves of the trees and grasses.

Briney inhaled a deep breath of purely the freshest air she could ever in all her life remember breathing in! The sweet perfumes of flowers and sun-warmed grasses mingled with the softer scents of tree bark and soil to such perfection that every inch of Briney's body was all at once rejuvenated. She felt as if the unsullied air were coursing through her arms, her legs, her fingers and toes. The sensation brought such an impression of newborn emancipation—an even greater sense of deliverance than she'd experienced in the previous days since Mrs. Fletcher's passing—that she found her nervous trembling had stopped. Mrs. Fletcher wasn't there to scold her or to tell her to slow down her pace or that she wasn't walking as a proper lady should.

Consequently, even though she feared her hurried manner of walking might find her shoes leaving blisters on her tender feet at the end of the day, Briney walked the dusty road toward the Horseman's property as swiftly as her happy heart determined she should walk.

In fact, Briney was so caught up in the beauty of the day and the feeling of liberation coursing through her that it seemed she'd hardly been walking any distance at all when an enormous red barn suddenly breached the horizon. Its bright roof seemed to beckon to Briney—as if calling to her in announcing adventure.

And as she topped the small hill before her, the expanse of the Horseman's success was obvious, and Briney paused to study the large red barn, its smaller counterpart, and other outbuildings— fenced corrals filled to near breaching with beautiful horses and such a wide vista of grass-covered land that it appeared as if Mother Nature herself had swathed the earth with green velvet for as far as Briney could see.

It was as truly breathtaking a sight as Briney had ever seen, and in that moment Briney was content that her heart had chosen to linger in Oakmont for the rest of her days—if for no other reason than to walk the three miles from town, crest the hill overlooking the

Horseman's property, and take pleasure in the beautiful view before her.

Thinking to herself that Mr. Kelley had indeed given her wise direction in seeking out the Horseman's help in purchasing a proper mount, Briney hurried down the hill toward the corrals filled with horses.

As she drew nearer to the place, Briney smiled as she noticed several men on horseback were mixed in among the horses being corralled. They whistled and called out to one another as the horses reared, whinnied, and bolted here and there within the confines of the corral fencing.

It was obvious these horses were not used to being corralled, and a part of Briney felt rather sad for them, for she knew what it was to live without being fully free.

"Howdy, ma'am," a young man greeted Briney as he approached from the direction of the enormous red barn. "Can I help you out with somethin'?"

"Well, I hope so," Briney said, returning the young man's friendly smile. "I'm interested in purchasing a horse, and Mr. Kelley in town told me that I should inquire of the Horseman, Mr. Cole, concerning the matter."

The young man's smile broadened. "Oh yes, ma'am! Mr. Cole is the greatest horseman in the state, I can assure you of that! He can match a body with the right horse in his sleep, Miss…uh…Miss…"

"Briney," Briney answered, offering the man her hand. "Briney Thress."

The fellow accepted Briney's handshake, grasping her hand much more firmly than she was accustomed to.

"Charles Plummer, ma'am," the young man said, "but most folks just call me Charlie."

"I'm very pleased to meet you, Charlie," Briney said, smiling. He was a very charming young man. Briney surmised his age to be that of near her own. He was tall, with bright green eyes that seemed to smile in unison with the smile on his lips, and he owned brown hair—at least from what Briney could gather from his hair showing from beneath his hat.

"Pleased to meet you too, ma'am," Charlie said with a nod. "Now, if you'd like to follow me over here to the main stable, I'll fetch Mr. Cole for you, all right?"

"Of course," Briney assured him as a small giggle of delight escaped her throat. The man was so naturally charming she found herself feeling rather giddy inside. Furthermore, she was about to possibly purchase a horse—her very own horse!

The excitement in her bosom welled to such an expanse that Briney found she had difficulty breathing normally for a moment. And as she followed Charlie into the biggest of the red barns on the Horseman's property—as the aromas of leather, straw, horsehair, and even horse manure entered her nostrils—Briney breathed deep of the essence of the stabling and caring of horses, finding tears of elation brimming in her eyes. She'd never been in an actual stable before—never been in a barn, for that matter—and all at once, she thought for a moment that it might be nice to sleep in a barn one night—to breathe the scent of straw and horses, listen to the quiet whinnying sounds the animals might make. Thus, the idea of sleeping in the Horseman's barn set fire to a new dream in Briney's mind—a new dream to join the list of so many others she'd secreted through her life.

"These here on the left are spoken for, ma'am," Charlie explained. "But most of these stalls to the right are for sale. And Mr. Cole's got more in the west stables as well. You just have a look around, ma'am, while I fetch Mr. Cole. I won't be but a minute, all-righty?"

"Of course," Briney assured the young man. She was so overcome with the joy she was feeling at simply being in proximity with such beautiful horses that she didn't care if Charlie took an hour to find Mr. Cole!

Charlie hurried away, and Briney stood, frozen in awe for a few moments. Each stall in the barn was occupied by a beautiful horse! She was overwhelmed for a moment by the pure actuality of it—that she was free form Mrs. Fletcher's grasp and standing in a barn full of horses.

She drew herself back to her senses quickly, however, and, determining not to be tempted into falling in love with a horse that had already been sold, began ambling along the row of stalls to her right. Every horse in every stall was magnificent! The first stall was occupied by a beautiful bay horse, the next by what she surmised from her reading was an Appaloosa. A lovely grey horse whinnied a friendly whinny at her as she passed, and she giggled with delight.

Pausing at the sixth stall down, however, Briney smiled. As was the fact with all the stalls, the upper part of the stall door was open while the lower half remained closed. A beautiful bay horse stood at the back of the stall, seeming to study Briney.

"*Sassafras*," Briney read aloud from the sign hanging on the lower part of the door. She looked to the horse in the back of the stall and smiled. "Are you Sassafras?" she asked, smiling. Instantly, the pretty horse hurried to the stall door and whinnied.

Briney was startled when the horse leaned its head out over the closed bottom of the stall door, nuzzling her with its muzzle.

"Oh my! Aren't you a friendly one?" Briney giggled. Uncertain as to whether it would be appropriate for her to pat the horse's head in returning the greeting, Briney shrugged and tossed caution to the wind. Reaching out, she tenderly stroked the horse's jaw and then its velvety nose. The horse whinnied again, shaking its head with apparent delight.

"She's right in here, Mr. Cole," Charlie said as he motioned for his boss to enter the largest stable on the ranch. "She's about the prettiest thing I've ever seen, truth be told, and dressed like she just waltzed outta some big society event. I wasn't sure what to tell her, so I just come and fetched you. I figured you best handle this one, bein' as I don't know her experience with ridin', and, well, I ain't never sold a horse to a lone woman before, boss."

Gunner Cole chuckled. "Oh, that's all right, Charlie. That last mustang 'bout tore me to shreds breakin' him. I could use a break."

But Gunner and Charlie both stopped in their tracks as they stepped into the stable.

"Is that Sassy nuzzling up to her?" Charlie asked in an awed whisper.

"Yeah," Gunner mumbled, too astonished by what he saw to say anything else. Of course, truth be told, Gunner wasn't sure whether it was the fact that Sassafras seemed to be taking to the woman who'd come to buy a horse or that the woman who'd come to buy a horse was young, pretty, and dressed in the most striking purple dress he'd ever seen anybody wear in Colorado.

"Is…is she plannin' on ridin' this horse she's gonna buy, do you know, Charlie?" Gunner asked in a whisper.

Charlie shrugged. "She didn't say for certain, but that was the impression I got," Charlie answered.

Gunner rubbed at the two-days' whisker growth on his chin. "Um…would you, um…would you run on over and tell Ike to keep breakin' them new mustangs…and then would you run on into the house and fetch me a shirt? I done threw away the one I was wearin'. That last mustang tossed me into a fence, and it wasn't nothin' but a rag after that."

"You bet, boss," Charlie said.

Gunner rubbed his whiskery chin again, mumbling to himself, "Well, this oughta be interestin'."

Briney heard the jingle of spurs approaching but couldn't seem to tear her attention away from the friendly horse nuzzling her arm. It wasn't until the person drew nearer to her and spoke that every hair on the top of her head tingled—that every inch of her flesh broke into goose bumps.

"Mornin' there, ma'am," the rich, smooth voice greeted, the same voice that had lulled Briney to sleep on several occasions since Mrs. Fletcher's death. "I hear you've come lookin' to buy a horse."

Briney found she couldn't speak as she looked to her right to see a tall, broad-shouldered man striding toward her—a tall, broad-shouldered man wearing only boots and a pair of blue jeans! He was bare from the waist up, and his torso was bronzed to such an extent that Briney suspected he often pranced around in such a state of undress.

Still, the fact of the matter was, not only was the man breathtakingly good-looking—dark-haired, blue-eyed, with a flawlessly square jaw and straight nose—but he was the man who owned the voice that had so often soothed her since Mrs. Fletcher's death, the voice she eavesdropped on when she was drifting off to sleep.

"You are lookin' to buy a horse, aren't you?" the man asked, striding to stand directly next to her.

"Why…y-yes, that's correct," Briney managed to respond, studying the man from head to toe in awed astonishment. Briney gulped a bit, truly trying not to stare—trying to keep her mouth from falling agape in awe of the man's unrivaled good looks and perfectly sculpted musculature.

"Well, you've come to the right man then," the man said, smiling at her and causing her knees to feel as if they might give way at any moment.

Offering his hand to her, he introduced himself. "I'm Gunner Cole. Some folks just call me the Horseman."

Placing her trembling, kid-gloved hand in his callused and obviously very powerful one, Briney managed to stammer, "Br-Briney Thress. It's a pleasure to finally meet you, Mr. Cole."

As Gunner shook her hand with firm confidence, Briney couldn't keep a smile of flattered delight from curving her lips as he said, "The pleasure is all mine, ma'am. I'm sure of that." Then he asked, "But I am curious as to what you mean by it's nice to *finally* meet me?"

Briney's delight turned to a knot of uncomfortable nervousness, and again she gulped. She couldn't possibly tell him the truth—that she'd been eavesdropping on his conversations with his friends at night in order to relax enough to drift to sleep. She couldn't possibly tell him that, as wonderful as his voice was, his physical appearance was even more magnificent.

She paused a moment, trying to look unaffected as she inwardly struggled for an answer. Yet it was difficult to think of one with him standing there, looming over her only half dressed—looking down at her with blue eyes through dark eyelashes that perfectly matched the color of the several days' growth of whiskers, accentuating the faultless angle of his jaw and chin. Now that he was closer to her, she could see that his hair was a deep chestnut that looked almost black where it showed beneath his well-worn hat.

At last, however, Briney found her voice and a measure of composure and answered, "Mr. Kelley, the proprietor of the boardinghouse in town," she managed, "he said you're the best horseman in six counties and that you would be the one to talk to about purchasing a horse."

Gunner Cole smiled, and Briney thought she might swoon at the euphoric effect it had on her. "Well, I don't know if I'm the best horseman in six counties, but I do love horses, and I do try to match the right horse with the right owner."

Briney exhaled a sigh of both admiration and relief. It seemed as if Mr. Cole would be willing to help her.

"Now, why don't you tell me a bit about yourself and the temperament you're lookin' for in a mount, Miss Thress?" Gunner began.

"Well, in truth, Mr. Cole, I've never owned a horse before, though I've ridden a great deal," Briney explained. She began to wring her hands, for the man so wildly unsettled her she was afraid she would forget why she'd sought him out in the first place. "So I suppose I should just say to you that…well, I'm a novice who has always loved horses from afar and always dreamt of having a horse of my own to ride…" She looked to him and bravely added, "To ride astride…and whenever and wherever I like. Therefore, I'm thinking I need a horse that is experienced and patient. One that will be tolerant of my learning to ride astride and things."

She was worried when Gunner frowned and studied her a moment. "You're a novice? Meaning…you're new in ownin' a horse, right? Not that you're gettin' ready to become a nun in a convent?"

Briney laughed—wholeheartedly burst into laughter. "Oh no! No, of course not, Mr. Cole. I definitely mean that I'm new to dealing in matters of horse sales and stabling." She laughed again for a moment, adding, "Oh, believe me, I'm the furthest woman from becoming a nun you've ever known."

Gunner Cole's handsome browns arched in astonishment then as he asked, "Really? The furthest from being a nun? Do you mean you're a...a..."

"Oh, heavens no!" Briney gasped, mortified as she realized what he must've thought she meant. "No! No! I just meant that...I've never had any intention of becoming a nun. I'm not even Catholic or anything! I just meant...well, I just meant that I'm an average woman, simply looking to buy and hopefully board a horse of my own."

Gunner's smile reappeared, and he said, "Well, good. Because I will admit that I don't have too much experience in matchin' up horses with nuns." He chuckled, adding, "No experience come to think of it."

The horse named Sassafras nuzzled Briney's arm once more, and she giggled. "This horse certainly seems to have a sweet character," she said.

"Oh, she does," Gunner assured her. "Here, take off them gloves you're wearin' and really give her some attention. Let's see how you two get along here for a minute or two, all right?"

"Well, if you're sure I should," Briney paused.

"I'm sure," Gunner assured her.

Briney stripped off her kid gloves, handing them to Gunner when he offered a hand in which to hold them.

The moment Briney touched Sassafras's velvet nose with her bare hands, she began to silently pray that the Horseman would allow her to choose this horse as hers.

"She likes you," Gunner said. "And you should be flattered because ol' Sassy…well, she's pretty picky about who she likes."

"Really? But she seems so sweet," Briney commented.

"Oh, she is," Gunner affirmed. "Just shy sometimes is all." Gunner reached up, combing his fingers through Sassafras's mane. "She's a very special horse, and I've been waitin' for just the right person to take her." He looked down at Briney a moment, his eyes narrowing as he studied her. "Maybe you'll be that right person, hmmm?"

"Oh, I hope so!" Briney couldn't keep from admitting. "She's so sweet! It's almost like she…well, like she likes me or something. Though I know that sounds like nonsense."

"Not at all," Gunner said. "I think horses are like people. They know when they've found someone who'll care for them as much as they care for the person. As I said, Sassy is usually pretty shy. The fact that she came right to you like she seems to have done…that says a lot." He paused and actually winked at Briney, adding, "It says a lot about you, Miss Thress." He stroked Sassy's jaw a moment and, speaking to the horse, said, "Me and Sassy, we go way back. I was there waitin' for her when she was foaled."

"Oh! Then she's *your* horse?" Briney asked, hoping the disappointment wasn't too obvious in her voice. She could see that the horse was special to Gunner, and she feared he wouldn't want to part with it.

"Nope," he said. "She was my mother's. Mama rode her up until the very day she passed."

"Oh, I see," Briney mumbled, stepping back from Sassafras. "I'm so sorry. I-I didn't realize that…"

But Gunner shook his head, saying, "Please don't misunderstand me, Miss Thress. It's not that I'm not willin' to sell Sassy. It's just that I've been waitin' for the right person to sell her to."

"Yes, but if she belonged to your mother…" Briney began.

Gunner leaned down so that his face was almost level with Briney's. "She was my mother's, but I think she's tryin' to tell us that she'd like to be yours now, don't you?"

Sassafras whinnied—nodded as if she agreed with what Gunner had said.

"You see?" he chuckled. "Sassy knows exactly what I'm sayin'."

Tentatively reaching out—for the truth was, Briney had already decided she wanted Sassafras and was so afraid something would keep them apart that she was afraid to hope too much—Briney stroked the horse's velvety nose.

Sassafras nuzzled Briney's shoulder and then touched her nose to Briney's cheek.

"She doesn't seem averse to me, at least," Briney commented.

"Nope. I'd say she's already chosen you, Miss Thress," Gunner said. "And if you decide to take her…why, this'll be the easiest sale I ever made."

Briney smiled up at Gunner Cole. He wasn't going to refuse to sell her Sassafras. In fact, it appeared as if he'd already made up his mind that Briney could, indeed, purchase the horse.

"Hey there, boss," Charlie called, appearing at the opposite end of the stable. Hurrying toward Briney and Gunner, he pulled up short when he reached them. "Here's you a clean shirt," he said, handing a rather faded red shirt to Gunner. He looked to Briney then, asking, "Have you taken a likin' to Sassy here then, Miss Thress?"

"Oh, definitely," Briney admitted.

"Good…good," Charlie said, obviously out of breath. "Ike said he'll take over breakin' that chestnut mustang, boss."

"Thanks, Charlie," Gunner said, slipping his muscular arms into the arms of the shirt Charlie had given him. "Why don't you go on over and pull out Sassy's old saddle? Let's see if it'll work for Miss Thress here."

Briney bit her lip with secreted delight when Gunner neglected to button up the front of his shirt before reaching for the bridle hanging beside Sassafras's stall.

"Let's saddle up Sassy and let you ride her a bit, Miss Thress," he said.

"Oh! But…but I'm not prepared. I didn't come dressed for…" Briney stammered. Oh, how she regretted not wearing the split skirt Bethanne had offered.

"Oh, that's all right, Miss Thress," Gunner assured her as he slipped the bridle over Sassafras's ears. He studied Briney up and down a moment and then asked, "You got your bloomers and what not under there, don't ya?"

"Well, y-yes, of course," Briney answered, blushing to the tips of her toes.

Gunner nodded. "Well, that's good enough for me and Sassy. We'll get her saddled up and send you two out for a bit. You did say you've ridden plenty?"

"Yes," Briney answered. "I've just never ridden astride."

Gunner chuckled and exchanged amused glances with Charlie as he returned carrying a saddle.

"Well, you don't worry a bit about that, Miss Thress," Gunner said. "Ridin' astride is as easy as spreadin' butter on warm bread. You mark my words—in twenty years or so, there won't be a woman in this country still ridin' sidesaddle."

Briney watched as Gunner opened the bottom door to Sassy's stall and led her out of her stall and into the stable.

He clicked his tongue and said, "Charlie here will saddle Sassy up for you today, but if you decide to take her for your own, we'll teach you how to do everything—saddle her up, brush her, and rub her down when you're through ridin'."

Gunner looked directly into Briney's eyes then. "Of course, I'd like nothin' more than to board her for you, Miss Thress," he said. "I won't charge you for keepin' her here. I just would kind of like to have her around, you understand."

There was emotion gleaming in his gorgeous blue eyes, and Briney suddenly understood that, although Gunner Cole wanted his mother's horse to be loved, to be ridden, he wasn't quite convinced he could completely give her away.

"I think that would be perfect, Mr. Cole," Briney said. "I don't know where else I'd keep her anyway. I've only got a room at the boardinghouse, and it wouldn't make sense to board her at the livery when this is her home." She reached out, placing a hand on Gunner's arm. "Are you sure you're even wanting to sell her to me, Mr. Cole?"

Gunner smiled. "I'm still workin' on that, Miss Thress," he answered honestly. "But I'll tell you this." He reached up, putting the bit in Sassy's mouth. "I haven't seen Sassy this excited about goin' for a ride in years. She likes you, and I want her to be happy. So you take her out for a ride—take your time too—and then we'll talk about whether you want to buy her." He winked at Briney again, adding, "And whether I'm ready to sell her, all right?"

"Of course," Briney said. She wasn't disappointed, however, for she could see that, even though Gunner truly wasn't wanting to sell Sassafras, he would if he thought it would make the horse happy.

Once Charlie had secured the cinch around Sassafras's belly, ensuring that the saddle was secure, Gunner nodded and asked Briney, "Are ya ready, Miss Thress?"

"More than ready, Mr. Cole," Briney assured her. Her heart was racing with the anticipation of riding Sassy.

"Do you want me to get a mounting block, or…" Gunner began.

"No. If-if you don't mind," Briney interrupted, "I'd rather you just taught me to mount her myself."

Gunner smiled with approval, and Briney's heart leapt in her bosom with pride in knowing she had pleased him.

"All right then," he said. Taking hold of the reins, Gunner lifted them over Sassy's head. "It's easy enough. Take the reins and a bit of her mane in your left hand, and hold onto them while you take hold of the saddle pommel on the right side there."

Briney did as instructed.

"Then turn the stirrup toward you like this." Gunner held the stirrup for her. "Put your left foot in the stirrup, and just sorta stand up in that stirrup until you feel like your weight is centered there. Then gently swing your right leg over the saddle, slide your foot into the other stirrup, and there you have it," he explained.

Briney did exactly what Gunner told her to do, and soon she found she had mounted Sassy quite easily.

"Perfect!" Gunner exclaimed. "Now wiggle your fanny a bit, and square that saddle up on her back so she's comfortable."

Although Briney did blush at Gunner's referring to her "fanny," she did as he said and could feel the saddle settle perfectly onto Sassy's back.

"Well done, Miss Thress!" Charlie said, clapping his hands several times.

"Thank you, Charlie," Briney giggled.

The desire to simply send Sassy racing from the stables was nearly overwhelming to Briney. But she knew she needed more instruction first. After all, Sassafras wasn't her horse yet.

"Now, you said you have a great deal of ridin' experience?" Gunner asked.

"Yes, sir," she answered. "My guardian made sure I was well trained in riding. But as I said, only in sidesaddle."

Gunner and Charlie again exchanged amused glances. "Well, I suspect it's much more difficult to ride sidesaddle. So you shouldn't have any problems at all, Miss Thress. And if for some reason you should lose your way on the road, Sassy knows her way back to the stable. So just tell her to come home and she will, all right?"

"Do you mean to say you're going to let me ride her...right now?" Briney asked. "By myself?"

Gunner smiled and laughed. "Of course!" Reaching behind him, he pulled Briney's kid gloves from his pockets. "Did you want your gloves while you ride?"

All at once, pure elation in feeling free exploded inside Briney's bosom, stomach, arms, and legs.

"No, thank you, Mr. Cole," she said. Then, reaching up and pulling her hat from her hair, hatpin and all, Briney offered it to Gunner. "And I won't be needing this either."

Gunner, eyebrows arched in admiration, accepted the hat, and Briney patted Sassy's neck and asked her, "Are you ready, Sassafras?"

The horse whinnied with impatience.

Looking to Gunner and trying not to be so thoroughly aware of how handsome that man was, Briney asked, "What is it you say out here? Giddyup?"

"Yep," Gunner answered.

"Then giddyup, Sassafras!" Briney giggled as she gently nudged the sides of the horse's belly with her heels.

Briney heard the laughter of approval of both Gunner and Charlie as Sassafras eased into a soft trot and then lurched into a gallop.

And, oh, it was more invigorating even than Briney had dreamed! As the speed of the horse caused the wind to tug and pull at Briney's perfectly coifed hair, she didn't give one whit if she returned to the Horseman's stable looking like a feral child—for this was freedom profound, and she meant to relish it!

"Well now," Charlie began, "I can't say that I've ever seen the likes of that in my lifetime before. You, boss?"

Gunner smiled, shook his head, and said, "You mean a beautiful young woman from the city, all gussied up in some slick, expensive dress, riding off astride my mother's horse with her petticoats flappin' in the breeze? Nope. Can't say I have."

Charlie chuckled and then asked, "How long you think she'll be gone?"

"Hours, more'n likely," Gunner answered. "That there's a woman who's never known freedom, I expect. And now that she's got a taste of it…we'll probably have to ride out and haul her on home by the hair of her head."

Charlie nodded. "Ol' Sassy sure did take to her, didn't she?"

"Yep," Gunner mumbled. "And she ain't the only one."

"What was that, boss?" Charlie asked.

"Nothin'," Gunner said.

"Well, I best be gettin' back to help Ike," Charlie said as he sauntered off.

But Gunner stood for a few long moments watching Sassy and her rider until they were only a bay and purple mirage on the horizon.

"I sure am glad she's not a nun," he said to himself as he turned and headed toward the corrals where the new herd of mustangs he and the boys had wrangled waited to be sorted out.

CHAPTER THREE

Exhilaration—pure, thoroughgoing exhilaration! That was what Briney was feeling. As she rode farther and farther away from the Horseman's ranch and stables, a sense of being rejuvenated, invigorated—of having new life breathed into body and mind—restored and strengthened her. She couldn't keep from laughing out loud, occasionally squealing with delight as she rode, for she'd never felt so happy before—never.

Not wanting to fatigue Sassafras too much, Briney slowed the horse to a comfortable walk. After all, the simple rhythmic clip-clop of the horse's slow-paced walk was as soothing to Briney's soul as the gallop was vitalizing. Briney closed her eyes and tipped her head back so that the sun shone directly on her face. Oh, it felt so good! The bright warmth rained down on her cheeks, drizzling a sort of tranquil calm throughout her being.

Then, all at once and very unexpectedly, an overpowering wave of mingled emotions began to well up in Briney's bosom. Tears filled her eyes, and they were tears not only for the joy she was experiencing in riding Sassafras but also of mourning for the loss of

Mrs. Fletcher. Tears of sadness for her younger self—the Briney Thress that had been orphaned at the age of three, left to neglect and misery in the orphan asylum, until the day Mrs. Fletcher had arrived and plucked her from a group of ragged girls, all of whom were hoping for escape. More tears came as Briney wondered at what had become of her friends at the orphanage who had not been rescued from hunger, cold, and abandonment the way Briney had.

Feeling the tears streaming over her cheeks, Briney allowed herself to continue to cry. Mrs. Fletcher had always maintained that tears showed weakness in a woman—that a woman should never allow anyone to know what her true feelings were, whether joyous or bitterly sad. And so Briney had spent many, many years burying her true feelings—weeping only when she was certain Mrs. Fletcher was sound asleep and would not hear her.

But no longer. Briney was not subject to Mrs. Fletcher now. She was all grown up and free, and she would cry if she wanted to, laugh when she wanted to, and ride her horse when she wanted to. And so she did.

"She's been gone a long time, boss," Charlie mentioned. "And she ain't never rode astride before?"

"Nope," Gunner confirmed.

Charlie shook his head with sympathy for the young woman who'd come to buy a horse. "Think she'll be too sore to walk back to town?"

"Yep," Gunner answered, grinning with understanding at Charlie. "But don't worry. I'll just hitch up the buggy and drive her on back. I'm hankering for a piece of Mrs. Kelley's peach pie anyhow."

Charlie chuckled. "Two birds with one stone, hmmm?"

"Yep," Gunner said. "I'll even bring you back a piece of pie if you like, bein' that I'll have the buggy with me."

"That would be mighty nice to look forward to, boss. Thanks," Charlie said gratefully.

The fact was that Gunner was a whole lot more worried about Miss Briney Thress having been gone so long than he was letting on to Charlie.

Mr. and Mrs. Kelley had explained the young woman's situation to him a few nights before when he'd been having supper at their restaurant. Seems the old woman who had been Miss Thress's guardian and traveling companion had given up the ghost and left Miss Thress all alone in the middle of nowhere. Well, at least left her in the very unfamiliar surroundings of Oakmont. It seemed the girl had no family, no home—nothing. And yet she'd come to buy a horse from Gunner.

Gunner shook his head a moment as he thought of the sight that had greeted him when he'd walked into the stables: Sassy cozying up to a stranger, a very pretty stranger—a young women with hair the same color as Sassy's bay and beautiful, bewitching eyes the color of a dark blue horizon before a thunderstorm. Sassy didn't cozy up to anybody—well, nobody but Gunner and Charlie. Sassy was shy. It had always seemed to Gunner that Sassafras had somehow known the day his mother had passed. Neither Gunner nor Sassy had ever been the same after that. And Sassy, in particular, had become withdrawn.

Therefore, as much as a part of his heart hated to see Sassy with another owner, the greater part of it was happy to know she'd obviously found someone who had captured her heart the very moment the horse had seen her. It seemed Gunner and Charlie wouldn't have to ride her as often to keep her exercised and cheerful.

And anyhow, Sassy wouldn't really be leaving home at all, being that Miss Thress would be stabling her with Gunner. Still, Miss Thress had been gone a long while—almost three hours, in truth.

But just as Gunner was considering saddling up and going out to look for Miss Thress and Sassy, Charlie hollered, "Here they come now, boss!"

Looking in the southern direction where Charlie pointed, Gunner felt his eyebrows arch in what was either astonishment or admiration—or both. There, on the horizon, were Sassy and her rider, Miss Briney Thress. They weren't riding hard at all, but it was obvious by Miss Thress's appearance that they had at some point in the day.

As the horse and her rider neared, Gunner could see that Briney's hair had lost every one of its pins. It hung long and free—windblown—looking exactly like the mane of the horse she rode. Her cheeks were rosy, and her nose was as red as a cherry. Most noticeable, however, was the change in the young woman's countenance—as if she'd just managed to escape prison and was basking in the euphoria of her newfound freedom.

Even from the distance Gunner could see she was smiling. And as she rode nearer and nearer, at last reining in before him, he realized a smile was spread across his own face as well. He figured there wasn't a man on earth that could resist smiling at such a sight as Briney Thress astride Sassy and looking more cheerful and beautiful than any woman ever had.

"Mr. Cole," Briney addressed the Horseman, "this horse of yours is perfect! As gentle as a butterfly and yet as strong and quick as Joe Cotton himself!"

Gunner chuckled and smiling at her said, "Well, I don't know if Sassy's as fast as Joe Cotton...but she is a good-natured, calm mount." He paused, adding, "The perfect horse for a lovely lady like yourself, Miss Thress."

Briney laughed, delighted by his flattery. "Oh, now don't feel the need to butter me up, Mr. Cole, because if you're willing to allow me to purchase Sassafras, I'll do it here and now...right on this very spot!"

"Well, I'm mighty glad you've taken to her, Miss Thress," Gunner said, stroking Sassy's jaw.

"Need any help dismounting, Miss Thress?" Charlie asked, offering a hand to Briney.

"Oh no, indeed not," Briney assured him. "And I will admit that riding astride is much preferable to sidesaddle...at least to my way of thinking."

However, although Briney managed a graceful dismount of Sassy, the moment her feet hit the ground, she knew she was in trouble.

"Oh dear," she breathed as she was immediately aware of a terrible soreness in her legs and posterior.

"We might should've warned you, ma'am," Charlie began, frowning as he studied her with concern. "If you've never ridden astride...well, ma'am, three hours is a mighty long time to ride if a body ain't used to it."

Briney looked up to Gunner Cole, trying to appear as settled and strong as possible. She realized, however, that her severe discomfort must've been more obvious than she thought, for Mr. Cole rather grimaced in sympathy and said, "I...uh...I didn't realize you were plannin' on bein' gone so long, Miss Thress, else I would've warned you about the stiffness you'll probably be feelin' this evenin'."

"This evening?" Briney asked.

"Oh yes, ma'am," Charlie interjected. "What you're feelin' now…well, that's just the beginnin' of it, I'm afraid."

"What?" Briney gasped, looking at the horse wrangler in astonishment. "How can it feel any worse than this?"

"Oh, I'm sure it won't be as bad as all that, Miss Thress," Gunner assured her. "And besides, I was plannin' on headin' into town here in a few minutes, and it looks like you rode up just in time to catch a buggy ride with me. What do you say?" Gunner paused, his handsome brows puckering with concern as he added, "Unless you're wantin' to walk all the way back on your own. I just figured, well…that you might have somethin' to get back to since you've been gone ridin' for near to three hours."

"Three hours?" Briney exclaimed. She had no idea she'd been gone so long. "Oh, I'm so sorry, Mr. Cole! You were probably thinking I was a horse thief or something! I suppose I'm fortunate you didn't string me up by the neck when I did return."

Gunner chuckled, and the sound caused Briney's heart to flutter. He was so handsome! Everything about him was handsome—even the way he laughed.

"Oh, not at all, Miss Thress," he assured her. "I know all too well how a body can get lost in the day and just ridin' out to peace and quiet. But it is well past noon, and I do need to get into town here pretty quick. So unless you really do want to walk on back—"

"Oh no! No, no! I would be very grateful to you for allowing me to accompany you in your buggy, Mr. Cole…very grateful," Briney assured him.

"I…um…well, if'n you don't mind it, Miss Thress, I can unsaddle Sassy, comb her down, see that's she's fed and watered and all…if you like," Charlie offered.

"Oh, that would be…that would be very benevolent, Mr. Plummer," Briney sighed. "I am quite a bit more worn out than I realized."

"I'm glad to do it, ma'am," Charlie said, smiling with unspoken understanding. "You have a nice afternoon, Miss Thress. And I'll look forward to seeing you again. Next time you come out, I'll walk you through everything you need to know about groomin' a horse, all right?"

"Thank you," Briney said.

Her legs were burning as if they were on fire! Her inner thighs were the worst of it; she felt that if she attempted to walk, she'd collapse. She'd had no idea riding astride would cause such strain to her muscles.

"Well, I'll go hitch up the buggy," Gunner said. He looked at her, and although he attempted to appear unaffected, Briney could see by the furrow of concern on his forehead and brows that he commiserated with her discomfort. "The outhouse is just yonder a ways…just there in the trees," he said, pointing to a small grove of trees behind him. "There's a rain barrel next to it if you feel like washin' the ride off your hands while I hitch up."

"Thank you, Mr. Cole," Briney said. Yet even as she looked to where the outhouse and rain barrel stood just a ways away, she wondered if she would be able to walk there and back to see to her necessities.

Again Gunner smiled at her, another amused yet sympathetic chuckle echoing in his throat. "It'll take me a bit to get the buggy ready…so take your time, all right?"

"Thank you," Briney said. She was blushing so thoroughly that she could've sworn even the hairs on her head were crimson with humiliation.

Mustering as much strength as she could, Briney started toward the outhouse. Her sense of humiliation expanded when she realized that no matter how hard she tried to walk normally, the soreness in her legs and posterior made it impossible to do so. She was miserable in knowing that Gunner Cole was most likely watching her hobble along—that he must think her the biggest ignoramus on the face of the earth for having ridden herself into such a condition.

Once Briney had managed to reach the outhouse and see to the necessities needing to be seen to after a long ride, she made her way to the rain barrel outside it. Happy to see a barrel full of fresh, cool rainwater with which to wash her face and hands, she was nevertheless horrified when she looked up to see her reflection in the mirror hanging above on the outer wall of the outhouse above the rain barrel.

She gasped at the image of the woman looking back at her, thinking it could not possibly be her own reflection. The face of the woman in the mirror was as red as a summer radish! Having so enjoyed the sensation of the sun on her face, Briney hadn't, however, expected to see such a red flush on her tender skin. And she certainly hadn't expected it to be so extreme. In addition to her now fiery complexion, her hair hung in a windblown tangle of confusion! She looked exactly like an illustration of a madwoman she'd seen in a book she'd once read—unkempt, disheveled, and even somewhat maniacal!

Appalled at her appearance, Briney frantically began combing her hair with her fingers. It was such a snarl of windblown knots, however, that she at last determined the only way to make it even somewhat presentable was to braid it. Hastily working her hair into a long braid, she finished washing the dirt from her face and hands, inhaled a deep breath of courage, and turned to make her way back to the stables.

The soreness in her body was worsening with each passing minute! How would she ever manage to make it through the rest of the day?

And then a realization struck Briney: she didn't have to! If she could just make it back to the boardinghouse (and she was sure she would, being that the Horseman had offered her conveyance in his buggy), then once she was back in the privacy of her room, she could simply collapse. It was an opportunity Briney never had before—to rest when she felt like resting, instead of having to wait for someone to give her permission to rest.

The thought brightened her spirits a bit. And when the Horseman appeared from the far side of the stables leading a horse already hitched up to a nice, comfortable-looking buggy, Briney smiled. She felt exactly as if some handsome knight in shining armor were coming to her rescue—and she couldn't wait to sit down in the buggy and not have to walk for a while.

"I thought you might be thirsty," Gunner explained, offering a canteen he'd filled with cool water to Briney. "And I figured that a proper lady like you most likely wouldn't be drinkin' out of the same rain barrel she'd used to wash up with."

The pretty young woman smiled and gratefully accepted the canteen.

"Thank you, Mr. Cole," she said.

Gunner watched as Briney drank from the canteen. He smiled, pleased and amused at how quickly she'd pulled herself back together after her ride. She'd somehow managed to work her windblown hair into a nice, tidy braid, and her entire countenance appeared refreshed—even for the state of her sunburned, albeit very lovely, face. The girl was no limp dishcloth, looking bright-eyed and bushy-tailed even for the fact Gunner knew her discomfort from the ride had to be severe.

"Water!" Briney sighed, screwing the cap back onto the canteen and handing it to Gunner. "There's nothing like it in all the world."

Gunner smiled, agreeing. "You'll get no argument from me on that point, Miss Thress." Reaching back to put the canteen of water on the floor of the buggy, he asked, "Are you ready to get on home then?"

"I am," Briney said, smoothing her dress as she hobbled to one side of the buggy. "This is a lovely buggy, Mr. Cole. And I thank you for the ride into town."

Gunner barely restrained a chuckle as he watched Briney trying to lift one small, booted foot onto the mounting bar of the buggy. It was so painfully obvious that her legs were stiffening worse by the moment, that her sunburn was deepening by the second, and that she was attempting to appear as if absolutely nothing at all were discomforting to her.

"I've got your hat and gloves sittin' there on the seat," Gunner said as he reached out, taking her waist between his hands and lifting her up so that her legs didn't have to bear the weight of her body. "You might wanna be careful not to smash them."

"Thank you," Briney said—and Gunner knew that if her cheeks could've been any redder for the sake of blushing, they would've been.

A quiet groan escaped her lips as she sat down on the buggy seat, and again Gunner had to silence the chuckle rising in his throat. He'd been sore on occasion after a long ride, and he could imagine how much worse the feeling would be to a soft, genteel young woman who had never experienced that particular pain before.

Taking his seat beside her in the buggy, Gunner clicked his tongue and gently slapped the lines at the horse's back. He heard Briney sigh with relief as the buggy lurched forward and they were on their way.

"I...I know my unsteady gait might seem to indicate otherwise, Mr. Cole," Briney began awkwardly. "But I enjoyed my ride with Sassafras today more than...well, more than anything I can remember in a very long time. Please do be assured of that, and of my sincere intent to purchase her...if you will allow me to, of course."

Gunner grinned. "Well, I'm mighty glad you and Sassy took to each other the way you did," he assured her. "And I will allow you to have her." He glanced to Briney and winked with guarantee. "It's been too long since she had another woman around to care for her."

Briney smiled with radiant joy, and Gunner was further struck by how amazing it was—the fact that she looked so becoming when her face was as red as a tomato and her hair still a bit frazzled.

"Oh, thank you so much, Mr. Cole!" Briney exclaimed with exuberance. "How much are you asking for Sassafras? I assure you, I am well able to pay for her and her keep in your stables."

Truth be told, Gunner would've gladly given Sassy to Briney—and fed and stabled the animal for free. Still, from what he'd heard, he knew the young woman was on her own and wanting to make a life for herself. Therefore, although he could not bring himself to name the true price of the worth of Sassy, and her saddle, gear, and stabling, he did manage to say, "I'll give you ol' Sassy for forty dollars, throw in her saddle for another twenty, and charge you a dollar fifty a month for stablin' and feed. Does that sound fair?"

"More than fair!" Briney exclaimed, clapping her hands together with triumph and excitement. "I can pay you as soon as we get to the boardinghouse," she continued. "I wouldn't want to risk someone else buying her, being as I may not be able to return to your stables to claim her for a day or two because of my…because I…I probably should wait that long before coming to ride her again…don't you think?"

Gunner's grin broadened. "Well, it might be a good idea to rest up a bit. And that'll give you a chance to get yourself a ridin' skirt and things too." He looked at her, winked again, and added, "And I would never go back on a promise of sale, Miss Thress."

"But what if someone else takes to Sassafras before I get back?" Briney asked, her concern still blatant.

"I don't operate my business that way," Gunner told her. He offered a hand to her, adding, "Will a handshake convince you that I'm in earnest?"

Briney's pretty smile appeared again. "Yes, indeed," she said, taking his hand.

Gunner's hands were strong, and his firm, reassuring grip was evidence of a man of high character. Briney savored the feel of his warm, callused palm gripping hers and felt let down somehow when he released it. The thrill that had traveled through her when Gunner had clasped her hand was a sensation she'd never experienced before—never! Of course, the soothing, safe feeling she'd experienced on the nights she'd been able to drift off to sleep while listening to the calming masculinity of the intonation of his voice had had a similar effect on her—but the pleasure of his touch was unmatched!

Briney found herself momentarily distracted in trying, in vain, to concoct a reason that might make him grasp her hand again. Before she could think of something, however—for she was lacking in flirtation skills (being that Mrs. Fletcher had forbidden Briney to flirt)—Gunner asked her a question, and her thoughts of somehow tricking him into touching her again were scattered.

"The Kelleys are mighty fine folks," he said, obviously offering casual conversation. "And they run a fine establishment. I'm particularly fond of Mrs. Kelley's cookin' at the restaurant."

"Oh my, yes!" Briney wholeheartedly agreed. "My room at the boardinghouse is so very comfortable, and Mrs. Kelley certainly is a wonderful cook. Why, she baked a batch of blueberry muffins the other morning; I swear I've never tasted anything so heavenly for breakfast."

"Yes, indeed," Gunner agreed. "Though I'm most fond of her pies…especially her peach pie this time of year."

Briney giggled with understanding and delight in agreeing with him. "It's too delicious for words! And when she slathers it with fresh, warm cream…mmm! I can almost taste it now. I must be hungry after that long ride with Sassafras."

"I would imagine so," Gunner chuckled.

There was silence between them for several long moments, and then Gunner began, "I understand you lost your guardian or someone recently."

Briney nodded. "Yes…Mrs. Fletcher," she admitted. She felt a blush of humiliation rise to her already red cheeks, but for some reason, she continued, "I suppose you know then that I was an orphan and that Mrs. Fletcher adopted me to be her traveling companion when I was just a girl."

"No, I didn't know that," Gunner admitted.

His handsome brow furrowed into a slight frown, and Briney sighed with disappointment. It seemed the handsome Horseman of Oakmont was as disgusted by orphans as most city people were.

"People don't like orphans," Briney thought aloud.

"They don't?" Gunner asked. "Why not?"

Briney herself frowned—studied him for a long minute before asking, "Are you in earnest, Mr. Cole?"

"What do you mean?" Gunner asked. He seemed sincere in his ignorance to the general population's thinking where orphans were concerned.

"Most people, at least in my experience, think all orphans are worthless, criminal types, not worthy of befriending," she told him.

His frown deepened. "Why would people think that?" he asked. "It's not a child's fault if their parents are lost...if they're left alone in the world."

Briney's heart leapt with gratitude, and her frown relaxed. "Well, your opinion is rare, Mr. Cole."

He shrugged broad shoulders and said, "I don't believe in judging a body by what their parents did or didn't do. Everybody had different circumstances growin' up. Some are real tragic." He shrugged again. "And there are those who grow up in such bad conditions that they fall into the same type of life they were born into. Still, there's plenty more that don't."

Briney smiled as she listened to Gunner speak—as she saw the sincerity on his face as he did.

"Take me for instance," he began. "One of my grandfathers was a Quaker, born and raised. And he married a Quaker woman, also born and raised. But his wife was meaner than an ol' wet hen and twice as cold...quite the opposite of the kind, nurturing Quaker mother my grandpa had grown up with. So one day my grandpa...he just up and ran off with the woman who ran a local brothel. He divorced his first wife and married the scarlet woman who'd owned the brothel. Of course, his second wife…she retired from her profession the minute she married my grandpa, and she and my grandpa had four sons, one of which was my daddy. Well, just because my grandpa had run off with a woman who'd once run a cathouse didn't mean my daddy did the same. My daddy grew up and married a preacher's daughter, my mother, and they were happier than any married couple I've ever seen since."

Gunner paused a moment, his eyes narrowing with near suspicion. "So do you think less of me because my grandma was once a harlot?" he brusquely asked.

"Why…why, of course not!" Briney exclaimed, although she was astonished that a man she'd only met that very day would share such a revelation with her.

Gunner nodded with approval. "Then why should people think less of you because you were once an orphan girl, hmmm?"

"Well…well, because they're…they're…" Briney stammered.

"Because they're malicious in nature sometimes…always trying to make themselves feel better about themselves by defiling the character of others. Ain't that the truth of it?" he stated.

Briney smiled. "So…you're not only a superior horseman and a fair businessman with a rare streak of integrity, but you're also much wiser than would be expected for a man under the age of eighty," she noted aloud.

Gunner chuckled. "Oh, all that flattery ain't necessary, Miss Thress. I already offered you a good deal on Sassy and her stablin'."

"No, I really do mean it," Briney said. "I admire your wisdom…what you've said about not judging everyone by the circumstances they were born to. It seems few people consider things as you do…as I do."

"Oh, I'm pretty certain you'll find that most folks in Oakmont think different than what you might be used to, Miss Thress," Gunner assured her. He laughed then, apparently to himself, and began, "Still, it's probably a good thing you fixed up your hair and things after your ride. Otherwise folks might suppose I had had my way with…"

When he paused, appearing as if he wouldn't finish his thought, Briney prodded, "Might suppose you had had your way with what?"

Gunner shifted uncomfortably in his seat and then answered, "Folks might suppose I hadn't done right by you where horse business is concerned."

Gunner figured the old crone that had adopted Briney when she was a girl had made sure her traveling companion had stayed pretty innocent to the ways of men. Otherwise, Briney probably wouldn't have ventured out to Gunner's stables by herself in the first of it. Still, things were a bit different in Oakmont than they were in most cities. If a woman went out and bought her own horse—especially alone without a chaperone—well, folks didn't really see anything improper about it.

Hell! He'd sold Widow Murphy a horse just the week before, and she'd come out to the ranch all by herself, and no one had thought a thing about it. Yet the Widow Murphy was gray-haired, with children already in their adolescence. Still, things were a bit different in Oakmont. People worked hard, and they gossiped less.

Gunner glanced at Briney. Besides, he thought, she was sunburned to near a crisp. It was obvious she'd been out for a ride in the sunshine—for hours. And folks in town knew Gunner was good man who valued his integrity and good character above all else. No one would think anything was suspicious about his returning Briney looking like she'd been dragged over the countryside with one foot caught in a stirrup. And if anybody asked him why Briney looked like she'd been ravaged, he'd simply set them straight about what happened: she came to buy a horse from him and got lost in the beauty of the day.

But when Gunner pulled the buggy to a stop in front of the boardinghouse—when Bethanne Kelley and her mother both gasped in horror when they saw the condition of Briney's face, hair, and clothes—he wondered for a moment if, for the very first time, his spotless reputation was about to get dragged through the mud.

CHAPTER FOUR

"Briney!" Bethanne exclaimed. "What on earth happened?"

Again, a blush of humiliation that was entirely indiscernible because of her sunburn rose to Briney's cheeks.

"You look like you've been baked to a crisp!" Mrs. Kelley unnecessarily noted.

"Seems Miss Thress is a real horsewoman," Gunner said. "She found the horse she liked, rode out, and Charlie and I were thinkin' we'd better saddle up and go lookin' for her three hours later. But she come back on her own."

"Three hours in the sun? Didn't you have a hat with you, honey?" Mrs. Kelley asked. Her expression was that of deep concern.

"I did," Briney admitted. She watched as Gunner hopped down from the buggy and made his way to her side of it. "But I wanted to feel the sun on my face, so I intentionally left it behind. It was careless of me, I know."

Briney groaned as she stood up from the buggy seat. It seemed the idleness of sitting, even for the space of such a short distance as three miles, had caused her already strained and sore muscles to stiffen so badly she wasn't sure she could step down from the buggy at all!

Having obviously accounted for the fact that the buggy ride would find Briney all the more miserable and sore, however, Gunner simply reached up, taking her waist between his strong hands, and lifted her down from the buggy.

"I've...I've also discovered the detriment of riding astride for three hours when one is not accustom to doing so," Briney explained as Bethanne and Mrs. Kelley continued to stare at her, with mouths agape.

Briney watched as Bethanne and her mother exchanged worried glances for a moment. But she was entirely startled when, all at once, the two women burst into laughter.

"Oh, you poor dear thing!" Bethanne commiserated through her giggles. "I'm so sorry...and I know exactly how you feel." She laughed a bit more and then added, "And I'm not laughin' because of your misery, Briney—just because, as I said, I've done the same thing...more than once, in fact."

"Oh, me too!" Mrs. Kelley added. "I don't know what gets into a body sometimes, that we lose track of what circumstances might arise from gettin' lost in the beauty of the day." She turned to Bethanne and asked, "Remember last summer, when we had all that rain and the mosquitoes were so bad?"

"Mmm hmmm," Bethanne affirmed, giggling as she nodded.

Mrs. Kelley looked back to Briney and explained, "Oh, it was a beautiful sunset one night, and I just couldn't resist sittin' out on the back porch to watch it. But when I woke up the next mornin', I was covered in bites. I mean, covered! I was so miserable—for days, I was miserable—and so swollen with mosquito bites a body woulda thought I had one ghastly disease or another."

"Mama looked like she'd been covered in pink polka dots, that's for certain," Bethanne said, smiling.

Mrs. Kelley stepped down from the front porch of the boardinghouse. "So you don't worry a bit, Briney," she said. "This isn't anything that a warm bath and a bit of extra rest won't take care of. Isn't that right, Gunner?"

"That's right, Mrs. Kelley," Gunner agreed. Briney glanced up at Gunner, her stomach bursting with butterflies as he smiled and winked at her. He was so handsome! So capable, so strong, so the stuff of fantasy!

"You'll be good as new soon enough, Miss Thress," he said. "And then you and me can see to Sassafras's official sale and change of ownership, all right?"

"All right," Briney answered.

Gunner nodded and smiled at Briney. Then he looked to Mrs. Kelley, saying, "I was hopin' you might have some peach pie just lyin' around somewhere, Mrs. Kelley. I haven't been able to think of anythin' else all mornin' long."

Sylvia Kelley's eyes widened with the delight of being flattered. "Of course I do, Gunner. You come on into the kitchen with me and sit down for a piece." She looked to her daughter, adding, "Bethanne, why don't you draw a tepid bath in the bathhouse for Briney? Let her have a good long soak to ease those weary muscles of hers, hmmm?"

"Of course, Mama," Bethanne cheerfully agreed. "It'll give me and Briney a chance to catch up." Bethanne looked to Briney—who stood exactly where she'd been standing since the moment Gunner lifted her down from the buggy. "Because it seems you did, indeed, find a horse to your likin', didn't you?"

"Oh, I certainly did at that," Briney said, smiling with joy in knowing Gunner had promised Sassafras to her. She could still imagine the way his hand had felt when he'd taken hers in shaking it in assurance that he would sell Sassafras to her and no one else. The memory caused goose pimples to race over her arms.

Standing there looking up at him, Briney was paralyzed in a state of awe. How could it be that the alluring man's voice that had so comforted her over the past week or more belonged to the Horseman—the man who would fulfill her dreams of owning her own horse? How could it be that this same man was so uniquely handsome as well? How could it be that his simplest touch—or even the thought of his touch—could send her heart racing and turn her knees to syrup?

Oh, Briney well knew what Mrs. Fletcher would've said. *A handsome face doesn't signify a handsome heart, Briney Thress. I sometimes think that men are the most lustful, heartless, depraved of all God's creatures. And even if they aren't, they're not to be trusted.*

It was why Mrs. Fletcher never allowed Briney to dance more than once with the same partner at society gatherings—never allowed anyone to come courting her. Well, those were the reasons she professed as to why she kept young men at bay where Briney was concerned. Of course, Briney had almost always known it was because Mrs. Fletcher had hired her as a traveling companion and indentured servant for herself and did not want to risk Briney falling in love and wanting to leave her.

Still, Briney wondered if Gunner Cole might melt even the stone-cold heart of Enola Fletcher, if the old lady had lived on. For, from Briney's experience, the Horseman was a man of outstanding character, as well as uncanny good looks.

Gunner touched the brim of his hat as he followed Mrs. Kelley into the boardinghouse by way of the restaurant door to his right.

"Miss Thress," he said with a nod. Then looking to Bethanne, he added, "Miss Kelley."

Briney watched him go.

She heard Bethanne exhale a heavy sigh and looked to her to see that Bethanne was watching Gunner leave as well.

"My, my, my," Bethanne breathed. "That man is sure somethin' to look at, isn't he?"

Briney smiled, amused to find that she wasn't the only young woman in town to think Gunner Cole was attractive.

"He's a tall drink of water, that's for certain," Bethanne added, smiling at Briney.

"A tall drink of water?" Briney asked, for she didn't quite understand the comparison.

Bethanne giggled. "Yeah…a tall drink of water," she began to explain. "It means that Gunner Cole is so good lookin' that lookin' at him gives you a thrill…like drinkin' a tall glass of water on a hot summer's day."

"Oh, I see," Briney giggled. "Well, he certainly is one then…a tall drink of water, I mean."

"Indeed," Bethanne said, "though, if you want to know a secret, Briney…I'm sweet on one of his stablemen. Mr. Plummer."

Instantly Briney's smile broadened. "Charlie? I met him just today! Oh, he is a kind and handsome man indeed…and very polite."

"Yep, that's Charlie," Bethanne affirmed. "Oh, he just sets my heart to racin' like a startled bird's!" Bethanne tossed her head then—as if she felt she'd revealed something too personal. "But that's neither here nor there. Let's get you out to the bathhouse so you can start soakin'. And Mama grows a plant out by the back porch that will soothe your sunburn a bit."

"Oh, that would be wonderful," Briney admitted. But when she started to take a step forward, the sore, stiff muscles in her legs and derrière violently protested. She gasped and stopped cold.

"Unfortunately, the best remedy is to kind of walk around a bit, Briney," Bethanne said, a sympathetic frown furrowing her lovely brows. "A soak will help and then maybe some rest too."

"Very well," Briney said as she started forward again. As she limped up the stairs as Bethanne held one of her arms to assist her, Briney whispered, "I guess I should be glad that Mr. Cole isn't still here to witness this, shouldn't I?"

Bethanne giggled, "You should be very glad. You look like a crooked old lady."

Briney giggled as well, again grateful that Gunner Cole had disappeared into the restaurant before he'd had another glimpse of her in such a ridiculously weakened state.

"Poor little thing," Gunner muttered under his breath as he watched Bethanne Kelley help Briney into the boardinghouse. "It'll take her a week to recover."

"Oh, I don't know," Sylvia Kelley encouraged as she set a plate of peach pie slathered in cream on the table at which he sat. Mrs. Kelley's gaze followed Gunner's out the restaurant window as the two young women disappeared through the front door of the adjoining boardinghouse. "Briney has surprised me," she said. "When she and Mrs. Fletcher arrived, I thought sure the girl had no mind or will of her own. But it was soon clear that she did; she'd just never been allowed to freely use them. But since that old biddy died," Sylvia nodded, "well, Miss Briney has really begun to come into her own." She looked at Gunner where he sat at the small table. "Like goin' all the way out to see you today to buy a horse; that took a great deal of courage and determination."

"Indeed it did," Gunner agreed. He smiled and, lowering his voice, said, "You shoulda seen her when she first come ridin' back in after that three hours. I swear, I couldn't determine the difference between the horse's mane and the girl's."

He chuckled when Mrs. Kelley laughed.

"And that tender, fried skin on her face—it's gonna peel right off…oh, and be sore tomorrow mornin'!" Sylvia whispered. "But it seems she enjoyed it."

"Oh, she did. She did indeed. And so did Sassafras," Gunner offered.

Sylvia frowned, looking at him in astonishment. "You sold your mama's horse to Briney?"

"Mmm hmm," Gunner confirmed as he chewed a delicious piece of cream-slathered peach pie. "Sassy chose Briney the very instant Briney chose her," he explained. "I never thought I'd see the day that Sassy would quit lookin' for Mama to come walkin' into the stables. But today…well, when I walked in and saw the way Sassy was cuddlin' up to Briney, I knew that horse was finally ready for a new rider."

Sylvia shook her head in admiration. "You never cease to amaze me, Gunner Cole," she said. "You and horses…it's like you can read their minds or somethin'."

Gunner shrugged. "Naw," he said. "I just pay attention is all." He smiled at Sylvia, explaining, "You pay attention to people, and I pay attention to horses." His smile broadened as he added, "Although I never met a horse that can bake a pie the way you can, Mrs. Kelley."

Sylvia blushed, and Gunner was glad that he'd pleased her with his compliment.

"Oh, now don't you be goin' on like that, Gunner Cole," she said, still blushing. "I already promised I'd give you another piece to take home with you…one for Charlie too. No need to soften me up with flatterin'." She patted him affectionately on one shoulder and said, "Now you enjoy your pie. I'm gonna help Bethanne draw a bath for Briney. I'll be back in a minute or two."

"Sure thing," Gunner said.

Once Mrs. Kelley was gone, Gunner exhaled a heavy sigh of pleasure—for her peach pie and cream were simply the stuff of heaven. In truth, one reason he liked Mrs. Kelley's pies so much—any of her cooking, in fact—was that it reminded him of his Grandmother Cole's—his grandmother whom he loved more than anyone beyond his own mother and father—his grandmother who had once been a madam in a brothel before she ran away to marry his grandfather. Yep, Gunner's Grandma Cole had been the kindest, most nurturing grandma a boy could ever have had. It was one reason he didn't judge folks by their roots or their pasts. His grandma had changed her life entirely—not the loving, nurturing ways she'd been born with but rather her circumstances and life of sin. And though there were a lot of folks that professed to be Christians—good, God-fearing people that preached repentance and forgiveness—Gunner's Grandma Cole had found that most never forgave others, only themselves.

Yet she'd been a happy, righteous woman for all the days Gunner had known her. Gunner's Grandma Cole had never scolded him for anything—not even when he tossed a ball in her kitchen, breaking her bone china teapot. She just enveloped him in her warm, soft arms, dabbed his tears of sorrow away with her apron, kissed him on the head, and explained that the teapot was just a thing—an object—

and that no teapot would ever be more important to her than making sure her grandchildren knew she loved and cherished them.

Nope, Gunner had never known anyone as kindhearted and as willing to do for others as his grandma had been, and he missed her. He'd missed her every day of the past ten years since she'd passed on.

As he scraped the last bit of peach pie and cream from his plate, he thought to himself that even he was a bit surprised that he'd told Briney Thress the story of his grandma's past. In truth, it was the sort of story that would cause most women to faint of shock, right there on the spot. But Briney hadn't. Her eyes had widened a bit, but that was all of it.

Maybe it was because, as an orphan, she'd known unkindness in her own life. Or maybe Briney just wasn't the sort of person to judge. But whatever the reason, Gunner still wondered why he'd told her about his grandmother at all. He thought it was to put her at ease about her being an orphan. But in his gut, he felt maybe it was more than that. Truth was, he'd been as instantly drawn to Briney as Sassafras had been—more so, in fact. Maybe the reason he'd mentioned his own family background was simply to see exactly what Briney's reaction would be—to see whether she would find a man who was the grandson of a once-harlot repulsive or not.

Gunner smiled and mumbled to himself, "Or not." Briney was as easy to read as any horse Gunner had ever met—he found most people were—and she hadn't been disgusted by him or his grandmother.

He wondered whether she were feeling any better, if Bethanne had managed to draw a warm bath for Briney, and if she were already soaking the soreness of her muscles. He hoped so, for he wanted her to heal quickly so that she could return to the stables to spend time with Sassy.

Gunner chuckled as a vision of Briney riding up on Sassy came to his mind—hair a wild mess of a mane, face as red as a summer beet, and looking as if she'd never been happier. There was a certain rare and wonderful beauty in a woman who could enjoy a ride so much that she abandoned any care for her appearance. In fact, in all his life, he'd only known two other women with that quality—the ability to toss inhibition to the wind and savor life no matter what others thought. One was his mother, and the other was his Grandma Cole.

"And when I think of the manner in which I just tossed all propriety to the wind, Bethanne," Briney said, slapping one hand to her forehead in consternation. "I mean...I rode off with my skirt and petticoats clear up to my knees! What he must think of me!"

But Bethanne only giggled. "I think the Horseman was quite impressed with you, Briney," she said. "I mean, look at it the way he must've—a very proper lady arrives at his stables dressed in her very proper attire." Bethanne paused as she struggled to comb a knot from Briney's long, very tangled hair. "And what does this proper lady do? Does she wilt like a spring violet in the summer sun? No! She finds a horse fitted to her and rides off confidently, careless of pride and prissiness...rides off to a three-hour adventure all on her own."

"Do you really think so?" Briney asked.

"Of course!" Bethanne struggled with another tangle of hair and then said, "I've known Gunner Cole for near to five years now, and I've never seen him display such obvious admiration toward a woman as he did you today." Bethanne smiled coyly. "And the way he lifted you from his buggy…as if you weighed no more than a butterfly."

Briney smiled, warmed all over by the memory. "And yet I was too miserable to really enjoy the moment." She glanced at the mirror in front of her where she sat at the small, simple vanity table. "I look like…I look like…"

"Folks around here would say you looked just like somethin' the cat dragged in," Bethanne finished for her.

Briney's smile faded. "I do! Oh, I do look just like a drowned rat! In truth, a somewhat roasted drowned rat."

"Oh, you do not!" Bethanne giggled. She smiled at Briney in their reflection in the mirror from her place behind Briney. "You're as lovely as ever you were. Just a little more pink."

Briney laughed, and Bethanne joined her.

Running the comb through Briney's hair one last time then, Bethanne said, "There now. It's all untangled, so let's braid it loosely and put you in bed for a nap. I'll wake you in time for supper. In fact, why don't I just bring supper up to you tonight? That way, you don't even have to dress for the day again if you don't want to."

"Oh, that would be so kind of you, Bethanne!" Briney admitted with a sigh. "I feel so tired and sore, and…my face feels like leather." Briney touched the hot, sensitive skin of her cheek, wincing—for it was truly painful to the touch.

"It will get better quickly," Bethanne assured her. "I'll bring some more of Mama's aloe vera plant up for you. It really does work miracles on soothing sunburned skin."

"Thank you, Bethanne," Briney said, capturing one of Bethanne's hands as she finished braiding Briney's hair. Turning to face her, she added, "You have been so kind to me. Your entire family has! And though it sounds rather morbid, I suppose…I am so glad that, if Mrs.

Fletcher had to pass away and leave me all alone, I'm thankful she left me here in Oakmont with you."

Bethanne leaned forward, throwing her arms around her new friend's neck and kissing her cheek. She was glad Mrs. Fletcher had died and left Briney there with the Kelley family too! For one thing, Bethanne had never had a close friend. Already she felt more akin to Briney than she had to any of the other girls of her age and acquaintance.

There was something *deep* about Briney; that's the only word Bethanne could think to describe what she felt when it came to Briney's character and heart. Briney had traveled the world, to places Bethanne could never imagine traveling to. Briney owned the beautiful, dazzling wardrobe of a wealthy debutante. Yet Briney didn't want to travel—possibly she'd never wanted to. All she'd ever longed for was a home and family. Furthermore, it was obvious Briney was more suited to the less stringent fashions of the American West than the fancy, frilly clothes Mrs. Fletcher had dressed her in. Otherwise, Briney wouldn't have ridden off on her own—skirt and petticoats up to her knees and careless of it for the joy of riding astride, and for three hours.

As much as Bethanne enjoyed riding her family's horses, the very idea of a three-hour ride struck her as being the stuff of boredom. So she figured Briney Thress had a tendency toward needing to feel free somehow—a feeling Bethanne didn't understand, for she'd always been free.

Yes, Briney Thress was deep to Bethanne's way of thinking—the kind of deep Bethanne had always heard her father use when talking of Gunner Cole. Furthermore, judging from the way Briney had unconsciously babbled on and on and on about Gunner the whole of the time Bethanne was combing her hair after her long, soaking bath, Bethanne's romantic heart had the sudden notion that perhaps the two very *deep* people in Oakmont might well be meant for one another.

Briney tried to keep the tears brimming in her eyes from spilling over. She'd never, ever had a true friend—not in all her life while living in the orphanage and certainly not in all her life in being the ward of Mrs. Fletcher. Yet the whole of her soul knew she'd found an everlasting friend in Bethanne Kelley—a true and loyal friend— and the sudden knowledge struck heart her with incredible force.

"Thank you, Bethanne," Briney said. "Thank you for…for everything…but most of all for being my friend."

"Oh no! You're not cryin', are you, Briney?" Bethanne said, holding Briney away from her and using the hem of her apron to gently dab at the tears in the corners of her own eyes. "Your face is already red enough, don't you think?"

Briney giggled, "I suppose so."

Sniffling, Bethanne stood up from the chair she'd been sitting in to comb Briney's hair. Taking Briney's hand, she said, "Now you just lie down a bit and rest. You'll still be a bit sore and stiff when you wake up, but you'll feel better by the minute, all right?"

"Yes, ma'am," Briney teased.

"I'll bring supper up at six," Bethanne promised.

"And if there's any of your mother's peach pie left…" Briney hinted.

"Then I'll bring that too, of course," Bethanne giggled.

"I really am sorry to be such a bother, Bethanne," Briney began.

"You are no bother, Briney Thress," Bethanne assured her. "Now get yourself some rest. I'll be up at six o'clock sharp."

"Thank you," Briney said.

"You're welcome," Bethanne said as she left the room, closing the door behind her.

Raising herself from the chair she'd been sitting in, Briney winced as her sore muscles made themselves well known once more.

"What in all the world was I thinking?" she muttered to herself as she hobbled toward her bed. "Riding for three hours when I'd never ridden astride before?"

Yet when Briney was resting comfortably on her bed a minute or two later, she sighed with satisfaction. As she closed her eyes, all that met her were visions of the beauty of the day—the feel of the warm sun on her face and the cool breeze through her hair, the scent of wild grasses mingled with saddle leather, and the rhythm of Sassafras's gait. It had literally been a dream come true for Briney— to ride out astride into pastures and hills where no one else was near.

And then—then there were the visions of the Horseman, Gunner Cole. As beautiful as her ride with Sassafras had been, not even the green vistas that met them had been as handsome and awe-inspiring as the blue of the man's eyes when he looked at her. All the warm sun on her face and wind in her hair hadn't felt as thrilling as the simple handshake she'd shared with him on the buggy ride home.

Squirming a bit until she felt as comfortable as possible, Briney lingered in memories of her first free-spirited ride, and of the man who had afforded it to her. She hoped her body would heal quickly—for as heavy as her longing to ride Sassafras again was, her yearning to again be in the presence of Gunner Cole was purely insatiable.

"Mmm!" Briney sighed with satisfaction as she swallowed another bite of cream-slathered peach pie. "Your mother's pies really are heavenly, Bethanne. Ambrosia for the soul."

"Oh, and don't I know it," Bethanne agreed, smiling. "My own pies are comin' along, but I can't get my crusts to be as soft and flakey as Mama's…no matter how hard I try."

Briney shrugged. "It's probably just because she's had so many more years of practice," she offered.

"Probably so," Bethanne agreed. She paused a moment, and a mischievous grin spread across her face. "Gunner Cole was just in at the restaurant for supper, and he asked Mama if he could buy a whole pie to take home with him. Seems he promised Charlie Plummer a piece and figured he might as well take a whole pie."

"He's downstairs in the restaurant? This very moment?" Briney asked as her heart began to race. She wondered if he would linger outside on the boardwalk under her bedroom window before heading home—converse with one or two of the other men in town the way he sometimes did.

Bethanne laughed. "Yes! But settle down or you'll pop your bloomer buttons! I do think your face just turned three shades darker of pink when I mentioned his name."

"Did I?" Briney said, putting her hands to her warm cheeks. "Is it that obvious that I find him…intriguing?"

Bethanne laughed. "Of course it is! At least, to me it is. But don't worry. Your secret is safe with me."

Briney sighed with joy and relief. "Just as your secret is safe with me."

Bethanne frowned, curious. "My secret?"

"Oh, I see you've already forgotten that you told me earlier today that Mr. Charlie Plummer sets your heart to racing the way Mr. Cole does mine, hmm?" Briney explained.

"Oh, I did! I had quite forgotten that I'd let that slip," Bethanne said, blushing.

Briney reached out, placing a reassuring hand on Bethanne's arm. "But it's all right…because neither one of us will tell anyone else each other's secret."

"That's true," Bethanne agreed. "Now, you just finish up that pie. I'll come get the dish and fork in the mornin'. You need your rest."

"I've been resting all afternoon, Bethanne," Briney reminded. Yet as she shifted her position in her chair, she knew her muscles would complain if she didn't just rest through the evening.

Bethanne smiled with understanding. "It's pretty miserable, isn't it? But you'll feel somewhat better in the mornin'. Once you're up and moving around, the stiffness won't be so bad."

"What an imbecile I was today," Briney grumbled. "Riding out like that for so long…and never having ridden astride before."

"Oh, don't worry so much about it, Briney," Bethanne encouraged. "The past is the past, and everybody does silly things once in a while. I'm just glad you didn't get lost or somethin'."

"I don't think I could've if I'd wanted to," Briney said. "I think Mr. Cole's horse would've known her way home from anywhere."

"I still can't believe he's agreed to sell Sassafras to you," Bethanne mused aloud. "Everyone thought he'd never sell his mama's horse. It's a miracle."

Briney smiled as she thought of the sweet horse waiting back at the Horseman's stables. "She just seemed to take to me the moment we met…and me to her," she explained. "It was rather strange, even to me…that she somehow chose me just as I chose her. Strange."

"Well, whatever it is, Gunner Cole must've seen it too. His mother loved that horse, and when she passed away, he wouldn't sell it to anyone who asked…no one. Of course, maybe two years makes a difference. Maybe Gunner has mourned as much as he needed and can let the horse go now."

As Briney considered Bethanne's reasoning, once more she wondered if she had mourned sufficiently over Mrs. Fletcher's passing. Oh, certainly she had shed tears and experienced a measure of loneliness of sorts. But the truth was, she didn't really miss Mrs. Fletcher, and she surely didn't miss being told what to do every minute of her life.

"Do you…do you think there's something wrong with me, Bethanne?" Briney asked.

"What?" Bethanne asked in return. "Whatever could be wrong with you?"

Briney shrugged. "Well, I still feel as if I should be more mournful over Mrs. Fletcher's passing. But I'm more relieved than anything…and continue to wonder if I'm just too heartless."

Bethanne exhaled a heavy sigh. "Well, your situation with Mrs. Fletcher wasn't one that anybody would miss. And maybe it's not even that. After all, you had to pull yourself up by your bootstraps and forge your way ahead in your own life."

Briney nodded. "I know. I just keep experiencing these flashes of guilt at not feeling worse about her death."

"Briney!" Bethanne sighed with exasperation. "She was as old as Methuselah, for pity's sake! She'd lived longer than most folks, and you took good care of her for the last ten years of her life! Don't beat yourself so. You mourned plenty and in your own way. Move on. Ride your horse, eat your peach pie, and sleep when you want to! That's my advice, anyhow."

Briney's spirits were lifted once more, and she nodded. "You're right...you're right. Her death wasn't my fault, and she was unfairly strict with me. She didn't beat me, but she didn't treat me well at all. So I suppose it's natural that I should feel some relief at her passing. I just had to be conscious of it is all. It does make me feel—"

"Enough," Bethanne interrupted. "You're beatin' a dead horse, and you need to stop. You've had a very tirin' day, and days like these tend to wear out a mind as well as a body. You need some rest and to let that sunburn heal a bit. You'll feel better in the mornin'." Bethanne's eyebrows arched with a rather daring appearance. "And when you're ready to ride out to the Horseman's stables to officially purchase your horse, perhaps I'll accompany you this time...just to give my regards to Charlie Plummer, you understand."

And with that, Briney nodded, and her mood brightened. Bethanne was right, and Briney knew that she'd resolved the matter two or three times already. It was time to move on and, as Bethanne said, quit beating a dead horse (although Briney thought the term rather morbid).

"You're right, Bethanne. You're right. And yes! You should come with me when I return to purchase Sassafras. That would be wonderful!" she exclaimed. "And if seeing Mr. Cole again wasn't already motivation enough for me to heal quickly—which it is— seeing you with Charlie will be!"

Both young women laughed together a moment or two before Bethanne took her leave of Briney's room. Once she'd gone, Briney sighed and finished her peach pie. Oh, it was good—in that moment, better than anything Briney had ever tasted!

And when she'd dared to actually lick the last of the cream from her plate (thinking how abhorred Mrs. Fletcher would be at such an action), Briney laid back down on her bed and waited—waited in hopes that when Gunner Cole left the Kelleys' restaurant downstairs, he would pause to say something—anything—so that she could drift to sleep with the sound of his deep, comforting voice humming in her ears.

Briney's heart leapt when, only a few minutes later, she heard him; she heard Gunner speaking to someone below her bedroom window. She sat up in her bed so that she could hear more clearly.

"Yep," Gunner said to someone, "I never thought I'd see the day either, but you shoulda seen that horse take to Briney Thress. A body woulda thought they'd known each other all their lives."

"But ain't you gonna miss that horse, Gunner?" Briney heard Mr. Kelley's familiar voice ask.

"Well, Miss Thress has agreed to stable Sassy with me, so I'll still have her right there," Gunner replied.

"It sounds like a good deal then, Gunner," Mr. Kelley said. "And I think your mama would be happy to know ol' Sassy's got a new friend. I'll tell you what, Sylvia and me, and Bethanne too of course, we really like Briney. There's somethin'…well, somethin' kind of unique and special about her. She's a fine young woman. Pretty too."

Gunner chuckled. "Yes, she is," he agreed.

Briney bit her lip with delight at hearing Gunner agree to her being either a *fine young woman* or *pretty too*. Her heart was hammering inside her bosom so hard she was sure the whole world could hear it.

"I hear you brought in a whole bunch of new stock," Mr. Kelley began. "Wild horses?"

"Yep," Gunner affirmed. "Mustangs. We rounded up last week, drove to my corrals, and we've been breaking horses every day since. My hind end is gonna be numb by the time we're finished. But I got the US Cavalry comin' through expecting to buy horses next month, so we've gotta get 'em ready to sell."

"Ooo wee!" Mr. Kelley exclaimed in admiration. "You sure don't let the grass grow under your feet, Gunner."

"I try not to, Walter. I try not to," Gunner responded.

"And I'm guessin' that pie is for your boys?" Walter chuckled.

Gunner chuckled too. "I figure it's the least I can do after a hard day's work—treat them to a piece of Mrs. Kelley's peach pie."

Briney listened as Gunner and Mr. Kelley conversed about simple things for the next few minutes. As ever it was, the sound of Gunner's voice was intoxicating to her senses, and soon she felt herself begin to drift off to sleep.

The last thing she remembered that night was the sound of Gunner telling Mr. Kelley to "have a nice evenin'."

Gunner exhaled a heavy sigh as he drove back toward the ranch. No doubt Charlie would be waiting with his tongue hanging out like a hungry dog in anticipation of Mrs. Kelley's peach pie Gunner had promised to bring him.

Gunner sighed again, thinking how much nicer the drive into town had been than the drive home. He'd been surprised to find himself driving the horse a bit slower than necessary when he and Briney were heading into town after her ride. In fact, it had taken him a moment to consciously understand that he was intentionally stretching the ride out so that he could linger in Briney's company for as long as possible.

After all, Mr. Kelley had been right: Briney Thress was pretty—very, very pretty. Furthermore, Gunner admired the way she'd just hopped on Sassy and ridden off for three hours without a care to anything else. It spoke of an adventurous spirit—of a strength and independence he immediately admired.

Laughing out loud, he thought of the expression on her face he'd managed to witness when she'd first seen her reflection in the mirror hung on the outer wall of the outhouse. Poor little thing had been mortified! But to Gunner's way of thinking, she'd looked all the more beautiful when she'd arrived back at the ranch with her hair a mane-tangle, her face as pink as watermelon meat, and her skirt pushed up clean above her knees.

Yep. Gunner figured Briney Thress was the kind of woman who could enjoy life, really enjoy it—ride out on a horse and not worry about whether her hair were perfectly coifed when she returned. As he continued thinking of Briney, an airy, breathless feeling rose in his chest for a moment—a feeling of admiration and intrigue—a feeling of wanting to turn his horse and buggy around, march into the boardinghouse, and demand to see Briney Thress again so that he could merely linger in her presence, gaze into her pretty sunburned face, and memorize every inch of it.

Of course, he couldn't return to the boardinghouse and demand to see Briney. Still, at the thought of the way she looked when she returned from her ride, his smile broadened again as he mumbled, "Poor little thing."

CHAPTER FIVE

"Thank you so much for coming with me, Bethanne," Briney said as the buggy ambled along its way out of town.

"Oh, believe me, it's my pleasure," Bethanne assured her friend with a wink. "I'll take any chance offered me to set my eyes on that cute Charlie Plummer."

Briney laughed, glad that her friend was gleeful with anticipation.

It had seemed a very long three days since Briney had ventured out to the Horseman's ranch in search of a mount and found not only the perfect horse for herself in Gunner Cole's Sassafras but also, and most infectiously, Gunner Cole himself—the manifestation of any woman's imaginings of the archetypal man.

For the past three days, as Briney had focused on tending to her sunburn and working out the stiffness of her sore muscles, all she could seem to think about was Gunner Cole—how entirely gorgeous he was, how strong and how wonderfully enthralling his voice was as she listened to him the past three nights consecutively as he conversed with different townsfolk beneath her window.

In fact, the more Briney thought about Gunner, the more rather desperate she grew to see him again—and not just to finalize the sale of Sassafras but also to simply gaze at him in awed admiration.

"You brought along your payment for the horse this time, didn't you?" Bethanne asked, startling Briney from her daydreams of the Horseman.

"Oh, indeed yes!" she assured her friend adamantly. "I'd have been a nitwit twice had I forgotten it this time."

And there was more to that way of thinking where Briney was concerned, as well. She'd thought of something during her three days of convalescing and daydreaming; she'd decided just where to hide the bulk of the money Mrs. Fletcher had left to Briney on her deathbed. After all, who would think to look in the corner of a horse's stall? Who would think to dig down deep enough to find a quart-sized canning jar or two filled with money?

Thus, Briney had decided that, once the sale of Sassafras was final, she would find a way to bury her money in Sassafras's stall. That way, no one would suspect she was about collecting coins or notes when she was rummaging around in her horse's stall—even if the Horseman did own the stall itself. Furthermore, she surmised that the stable hands, or even Gunner Cole himself, would never stumble upon money buried fairly deep in a stall that had housed the same horse for who knew how many years! Sassafras's stall was the safest place Briney could think of, as well as the one place no one would ever think to look for treasure.

"I like that ridin' skirt on you, Briney," Bethanne complimented as she studied her friend. "It fits you perfectly."

"Thank you," Briney said, smoothing the brown riding skirt Bethanne had gifted her. "Believe me, I got the better deal of the two of us. When I warned you that my blue frock is overly warm, I meant it."

"Well, winter here can get pretty cold," Bethanne offered. "And I plan on saving it for the holiday dance anyway…Christmastime, when I'm usually freezin'."

"It looks much better on you than it ever did me, and I'd much rather ride a horse than have an extra gown hanging in my wardrobe that might never be worn again," Briney said. "It worked out so well for us both." She glanced down at her brown riding boots she'd purchased at the general store. "And I do so love these new boots! My toes feel positively free in them!"

Bethanne giggled. "Yes, I've noticed those toe-pinchers you've been wearin'. I don't know how you tolerated them for so long."

Briney shrugged. "I never knew there were shoes or boots that were comfortable, so I never knew to resent them."

"Makes sense," Bethanne remarked. "Sad sense…but sense all the same."

Both young ladies laughed, and Bethanne hurried the horse pulling the buggy to a quicker pace.

The closer they drew to the Horseman's ranch, the faster Briney's heart began to beat. She'd been such a frazzled mess of sunburns and knotted hair the last time she'd seen him that she hadn't been able to truly savor the wonder of the man. Yet as she'd been resting up and preparing to travel out to meet him once more, the marvel that he was had seeped deeper and deeper into her very soul.

And when, at long last, Bethanne pulled the horse and buggy to a halt just outside the Horseman's largest stable, Briney was breathless with anticipation.

Much to Bethanne's obvious delight, it was Charlie who hurried over to greet them.

"Well, good mornin', ladies!" Charlie greeted. Briney bit her lip to stifle a giggle as Bethanne's eyes widened to the size of dinner plates, sparkling like they'd somehow sucked up every star in the heavens into them to shine for Charlie Plummer alone.

"Good mornin', Mr. Plummer," Bethanne greeted.

Charlie nodded to Bethanne and then to Briney. "I suppose you ladies have come to see to the finalizin' of Sassafras's ownership, hmm?"

"Yes, we have," Briney answered. "Is her owner around close perhaps?"

She was afraid her heart would leap right out of her chest somehow, as Gunner Cole stepped out of the stable, dusting off the weathered pair of chaps he was wearing.

"Good mornin', ladies," he greeted as well.

Briney felt goose pimples breaking over her arms and legs in unison with the rhythmic ching-ching of the spurs he wore at the heels of his boots.

"You ready to buy a horse, Miss Thress?" he asked as he leaned on the front of the buggy, looking up at her with a broad, dazzling smile spread across his handsome, oh, so handsome face.

"Yes, I certainly am, Mr. Cole," she answered.

"Well, come on down and let's get it done, shall we?"

He offered her his hand, and she grasped it as she stood up from the buggy seat. The warmth of his firm grip caused her to tremble a bit, and she hoped he hadn't noticed.

Briney stepped down and couldn't keep herself from pausing in staring up at him a moment. He was far more attractive even than she remembered!

"Why don't you let me take care of your rig for you, Miss Kelley?" she heard Charlie say to Bethanne. "Would you like a glass of water while Mr. Cole and Miss Briney take care of their business?"

"Why yes! Thank you, Mr. Plummer," Bethanne warmly answered.

"Looks like that sunburn you took on the other day is just about gone already," Gunner said, smiling down at Briney with such an alluring twinkle in his eye, it made her stomach flutter.

"Yes. Yes, it did—thanks in great part to Mrs. Kelley's aloe vera plant," Briney managed.

"Mmm hmm," Gunner agreed.

Briney nearly fainted when next the alluring Horsemen reached out, softly caressing her cheek with the back of one hand.

"Good as new and at least as soft," he said, winking at her.

Briney had to stiffen her legs—silently command her knees not to buckle under the euphoric sensation washing over her because of his touch. She was speechless, of course—entirely struck mute by the thrill racing through her.

"Well, let's get to horse business then," Gunner said. "We ain't gonna get you set up with Sassy by just standin' around, now are we?"

"No…no, I suppose not," Briney stammered.

Gunner stepped aside, motioning that Briney should precede him into the stables. "After you," he said.

Briney managed a glance at Bethanne as she walked past her—Bethanne, who stood mouth somewhat agape, obviously having been as astonished as Briney had been by Gunner's rather flirtatious gesture.

As Briney stepped into the stables, comforting aromas—of straw and leather, horsehair and feed—filled her lungs. It was wonderful—

all of it—the sunlight beaming through the stable windows, the rows of stables filled with magnificent horses. And then when Briney heard a neighing that was at once familiar, her heart leapt with even more joy.

"You see that?" Gunner chuckled, nodding toward Sassafras's stall. "I think she's been wonderin' where you've been. Look how happy she is to see you."

"Oh, I'm certain she's just happy to see you, Mr. Cole," Briney said—even as hope swelled in her bosom that Sassafras really did recognize her.

"Nope. It's you," Gunner assured her. "Go on," he urged. "You go on and greet her first. You'll see."

Somewhat tentatively—for she was secretly afraid that the Horseman was wrong in his estimation of exactly whom Sassafras was pleased to see—Briney strode to Sassafras's stall. Her anxieties were vanquished, however, when the horse immediately neighed in greeting her—even nuzzling her shoulder as Briney reached out, stroking its jaw on each side with her gentle hands.

"You really are glad to see me, aren't you, Sassafras?" Briney giggled with delight.

"Every once in a great while, I see a horse take to someone this way," Gunner said, striding over to stand with Briney and giving Sassafras an affectionate pat on the neck. "It always worries me a bit—puts me to fearin' the owner won't love the horse as much as the horse loves the owner."

"Well, that certainly isn't the case with me, Mr. Cole," Briney said. "I promise you that."

"Oh, I'm not worried about you, Miss Thress," he assured her. "I could tell from the minute I walked in here and saw you with Sassy that you were the woman to have her."

Briney looked from Sassafras to Gunner, gazing into his bluest of blue eyes. "And I won't disappoint you. I'll be here as often as you'll allow me to be."

Gunner thought about saying, *Well, I got an extra room in the house. Why don't you just move on in?* But he knew that, not only was it far, far from appropriate, it might just scare the girl off for good—Sassafras or not!

Therefore, instead he said, "You come down whenever you like, Miss Thress. If you have the time, I can show you how to saddle her up today. It'll take a bit of practice, but you'll be on your own soon enough."

"And will you eventually instruct me on helping to clean out her stall, as well?" Briney asked, surprising Gunner quite thoroughly.

"Well…well, sure, if you like," he answered. "We usually do all that for you, bein' that you'll be payin' to stable her here."

"Oh, I know," Briney assured him. "It's just something I'd like to know how to do—to better myself and so Sassafras will have every confidence and trust in me."

Gunner's smile broadened as he studied Briney. It seemed there was just more and more all the time to like about her. No one, not one person who stabled a horse with Gunner, had ever wanted to muck out the animal's stall before. Yet there next to him stood the prettiest, kindest, most amusing young woman he'd ever been acquainted with, and she sincerely wanted to learn to do the job herself. Again Gunner's breath seemed to catch in his chest as he studied her. He liked Briney Thress more and more with every passing second. And he found that it elated him more than it concerned him. After all, she was a different sort of woman than others he'd known. He was thinking that, with Briney Thress, there wasn't any pretense at all; she was exactly what she appeared to be—remarkable!

"So I've brought the money I owe you," Briney began, reaching into the reticule that hung from her wrist. Withdrawing both paper money and coins, she offered them to Gunner, saying, "Forty dollars for Sassafras, twenty dollars for her saddle, and one and fifty cents for her first month's stable fees."

Against his strongest desire, Gunner accepted the money from her. He knew it was important to Briney that she actually pay for the horse—although he would've willingly given Sassafras to her. Briney needed ownership—full, irrefutable ownership—and so she would have it.

Gunner reached into his shirt pocket and withdrew a folded piece of paper. "Here you go then, Miss Thress. A bill of sale for Sassafras and her rig. She officially belongs to you now."

Gunner laughed when Briney squealed with delight, actually threw her arms around his neck, and hugged him with excitement and gratitude.

"Thank you so very much, Mr. Cole! So very much!" she chirped. "You have no idea how important this is to me. Thank you!"

He couldn't resist returning her embrace—and found himself far more affected by the experience than he'd expected to be. So much so, in fact, that he didn't want to release her—wanted to linger in feeling her slight form enveloped in his arms and held against his body.

Therefore, when Briney released him, beginning to shyly step back, Gunner held her captive in his arms for a moment—just long enough to smile and mumble, "You're welcome," as he gazed down into her lovely blue eyes.

Briney blushed as he did at last release her—Gunner's assurance that she had indeed enjoyed his flirting.

Briney's entire body was simply covered in goose pimples! The moment she'd thrown her arms around Gunner's neck in appreciation, she knew she'd acted improperly. However, his response to her—the way he not only returned her embrace but also held her in his arms a moment, even after she'd released him, indicated that he'd enjoyed her gratitude.

Tucking a loose strand of hair behind her ear and nervously smoothing her riding skirt, Briney stammered, "Well, I…well…I suppose you should begin my training on how to saddle Sassafras now, shouldn't you?"

"I suppose I should," Gunner affirmed, "especially if you plan on enjoyin' a ride with her today, hmmm?"

Oh, that voice of his—that deep, alluring, warm, and syrupy voice! It completely weakened Briney's knees, and for a brief instant, one that entirely unsettled her, Briney wondered. If Gunner's voice was so affecting to her senses—if his touch sent her feeling like butter in a hot skillet—what in all the world would his kiss do to her?

Immediately, the memory of Mrs. Fletcher's strict adherence to propriety interrupted Briney's romantic notions where Gunner was concerned. Briney thought that if Mrs. Fletcher were, by chance, already in her grave, she was certainly rolling in it with cutting disapproval.

Still, Mrs. Fletcher wasn't there to scold Briney or to send her away from Gunner on some meaningless errand to ensure there was no idle time in Briney's life. Therefore, Briney pushed any worries about what Mrs. Enola Fletcher might be thinking from her place up in heaven and determined to focus solely on what Gunner was going to teach her about saddling Sassafras. It was a wildly liberating feeling that rose in Briney at the returning realization that she was at last independent—a free woman who could make her own decisions in life now. Furthermore, she decided then and there on the spot that if she were ever fortunate enough to find another occasion on which to offer Gunner Cole an embrace, she certainly would act on it—for he surely was accepting enough of the gesture, after all.

"Well, let's get to it then, Miss Thress," Gunner said.

Briney was rendered breathless then as Gunner actually took hold of her hand and led her to a nearby group of spacious shelves, each shelf housing blankets, bits, bridles, stirrups, a saddle, and so forth.

"This shelf here," Gunner began, letting go of her hand, "this is where I've always kept Sassy's tack. Everything you need when you're tackin' up is right here. So if it's all right with you, we'll just keep it that way. I figure it will be easier for you to keep it where it's been for so long. Do you agree?"

"Of course," Briney assured him. In truth, she'd never saddled a horse herself before and could only assume that "tacking up" meant to ready the horse for riding.

"I'm actually gonna just talk you through it, bein' that I feel it's better for the rider to learn to saddle up by puttin' his or her hands right there in it from the beginnin'," Gunner explained.

"Wise thinking," Briney said. Then, rubbing her hands together with excitement and to indicate willingness to work, she added, "Just tell me what to do."

Gunner smiled. The girl was entirely too fascinating for her own good. And he decided something right then and there—decided to take the risk of imposing on her, just for the opportunity to linger in her company a while longer.

And so he said, "I've actually got to ride out and check some fence lines today. Would you mind if I tacked up alongside you and rode with you for a ways? That way you can see exactly what I'm doin' while you're doin' the same."

Briney's eyes widened with delight. Her cheeks pinked up too, and Gunner exhaled a quiet sigh of relief in seeing that she was pleased by his suggestion.

"Oh, that would be wonderful, Mr. Cole. Thank you so much!" she exclaimed.

"And why don't you drop that Mr. Cole business and call me Gunner?" he suggested with a wink. "And I'll just take the liberty of callin' you Briney, if I may."

"Oh, of course you may," she rather squeaked. "Gunner," she added as her blush darkened from a pink to a cherry red.

"All-righty then, Briney," Gunner said. "Let's get these horses ready to ride."

"Nope," Charlie said to Bethanne as they stood watching the interaction between Gunner and Briney from just outside the stable. "I ain't never seen the boss look so…approvin' of a woman before. I think he's plain out sweet on your friend Miss Thress, Miss Kelley."

Bethanne smiled, placed a gentle hand on Charlie Plummer's arm, and said, "I think you're right, Mr. Plummer—or have we known each other long enough that I can call you Charlie?"

Charlie looked down into Bethanne's face, and her heart fluttered wildly as he answered, "Why, we have indeed, Bethanne. We have indeed."

Briney had thought there could be no more wonderful a thing than riding out alone on her very own horse. At least, that was her thinking before she knew the bliss of Gunner Cole riding with her!

Gunner was riding a newly trained—or, as he called it, "a green-broke" horse—and Briney was simply amazed at his handling of the animal. Gunner was truly a horseman—and not just because he bred and raised his own horses, rounded up and broke wild horses, and bought and sold horses. No, to Briney's way of thinking, what made Gunner Cole a horseman (*the* Horseman, as people in town referred to him) was the incredible respect, understanding, love, and compassion he held for the animals. He wasn't cruel to the green-broke mustang he was riding—firm, but never cruel.

In fact, during the course of their conversation together during their ride, Gunner had said, "The truth is, if I could just own horses and ride them myself—have miles and miles of pastures for them, stables, and everythin' the like—I wouldn't break the wild ones at all. I'd just let 'em run so I could watch them day in and day out." He'd shrugged, adding, "But a man has to make a livin', and I train the wild ones with patience so that at least they don't get bullied and beaten by the Cavalry trainin' them themselves. It still keeps me awake some nights, but I do what I must."

Briney had been touched, deeply touched, by Gunner's concern for the horses he broke and sold. And she understood how he felt, to a small measure. For if Mrs. Fletcher hadn't found a kind piece of her heart near the end, Briney would've been left entirely penniless. The only skill she owned with which to possibly earn a living was her piano playing. And Oakmont didn't have nearly enough people in it for a woman to make a living as a piano teacher. For all Briney knew, she might have had to play piano in the saloon or some such terrible place in order to provide for herself. Therefore, she understood that Gunner did have to sell horses in order to afford to own them.

They'd been riding together for some time when a fence line appeared. "Come on," Gunner said, dismounting and securing the reins of his horse to a strong fence post. "You'll like this."

Briney smiled and, without inquiring what it was she would like, dismounted and secured Sassafras's reins as well.

"Come on!" Gunner called to a group of horses standing a distance behind the fence. "You girls, you come on over here," he said as several beautiful horses began making their way toward him.

These were some of the most beautiful horses Briney had ever seen! A beautiful black horse was the first to reach Gunner, followed by a buckskin, a palomino, and a bay. Soon four horses were nuzzling Gunner, vying for his attention, strokes of approval, and the bits of carrots Briney realized he had in one pocket.

"These are my girls," he explained, smiling the most dazzling smile Briney had seen him don yet. It caused butterflies to flutter in her stomach—to see him so obviously pleased.

"Your girls?" Briney asked, reaching out to stroke the velvet nose of the black. "I take it they're special. Is it because they're so beautiful?"

Gunner chuckled. "It's one reason," he admitted. "But you see, these girls have all been bred with Stackhouse, my thoroughbred stud. He's stabled right now, 'cause he can be an ornery thing. But the girls here, I figure they'll all foal in about January," he explained.

"So their foals...they'll be worth a great deal of money?" Briney asked, patting the palomino's jaw.

"Their foals will make fine ranch horses," he admitted. He paused as a sleek, stunning sorrel mare trotted up to greet him. "But this little beauty...this is Brown Bonnie. She's a thoroughbred as well. So bein' that Stackhouse was sired by Old Billy himself and Brown Bonnie's sire was Buster Pray—"

"The racehorse?" Briney exclaimed.

Gunner nodded with approval. "Yes, ma'am, the racehorse."

"Oh, I've read about Buster Pray…and Old Billy," Briney said, awed as Brown Bonnie approached her. She patted the horse's nose, shaking her head in admiration. "So you're hoping she'll foal a racehorse."

But Gunner shrugged. "Not necessarily," he said. "But she's bound to foal a beauty, with strength and speed to boot." He exhaled a sigh of satisfaction. "Can you just imagine ridin' such an animal as Brown Bonnie's foal is bound to be? I tell you, I can't wait for the chance."

Briney watched as Gunner fed the rest of the carrots from his pocket to "his girls." Then he dusted off his hands and said, "You girls be on your way now. Go on," and a few of the horses turned to trot out across the pasture. The black and Brown Bonnie, however, lingered, and as Briney turned from them, she felt one of the horses nudge her back with enough force to cause her to stumble forward, directly into the arms of Gunner Cole.

"Oh!" she gasped as Gunner helped her to stand. "I…I'm so sorry," she stammered, blushing to the tips of her toes.

Gunner smiled down at her, keeping his arms around her much, much longer than was necessary for her to get her footing. "I might should've mentioned—Brown Bonnie…she can be a bit playful at times."

"I see," Briney managed to whisper, gazing up into the smolder of Gunner's narrowed blue eyes. She wondered for a moment how blue eyes could smolder, but smoldering was exactly what Gunner's eyes were doing—and she felt a thrill of euphoria race through her.

"You all right?" he asked.

"Mm hmm," she assured him with a nod.

To her great disappointment, he released her then, saying, "Well, I figure we've been out ridin' for close to an hour and a half. You ready to ride on back to the stables for now? I wouldn't want to wear you out and have you stiff as a board again, now would I?"

Blushing with mild humiliation at his reference to the condition she'd ridden herself into the last time she'd seen him, she nodded. "I suppose that would be the wise thing to do."

"It would," he agreed. "And that way, you can come back tomorrow if you like…instead of havin' to rest up for a few more days."

"You're a wise horseman indeed," she teased.

"And besides," he continued, "I still need to show you how to take care of Sassy after a ride, now don't I?"

Grinning down at her, he reached out, gently tugging at the brim of the hat she was wearing to protect the tender and still somewhat pink skin on her face. "I like this hat," he said. "It's kept your pretty little face from gettin' too much sun again."

Briney thought she would swoon as Gunner caressed her cheek with the back of his hand, sending goose pimples rippling over her arms and legs.

"Now, let's get you back so Sassy can get some pamperin'. What do you say?" he asked, winking at her.

"Yes," Briney managed to breathe.

Gunner helped her mount Sassy, and Briney was glad he did—for her legs felt as limp as overcooked string beans! Her heart was beating so hard she was afraid it would wear itself out, and she still couldn't draw an even breath. The man was purely intoxicating!

"You ready?" Gunner asked once he'd mounted his horse as well.

Briney smiled and nodded her assurance, and Sassafras followed suit as Gunner's horse broke into a dead run at Gunner's urging.

Briney felt the wind blow the hat from her head but knew the chin string would keep it from being lost as she reveled in the feel of racing across the meadow before them. Life was glorious, horses were beautiful creatures, and Briney was falling in love with the Horseman, Gunner Cole.

CHAPTER SIX

"And he asked if he could come callin' on me and my parents this Saturday evenin'!" Bethanne exclaimed with excitement.

"Oh, Bethanne! That's wonderful!" Briney giggled as the horse pulling the Kelleys' buggy clip-clopped back toward town.

"It is, isn't it?" Bethanne sighed. "And it's all thanks to you, Briney—you and your wantin' a horse of your own. I would never have had a reason to travel out to the Horseman's place and talk to Charlie Plummer if it hadn't been for you and your horse."

But Briney shook her head. "Oh, I think Charlie Plummer would've eventually found his way to you one way or the other, Bethanne," she playfully argued. "He's had eyes for you long before today. That was plain to see."

Bethanne blushed with delight. Then, being the courteous, caring young woman she was, she asked, "But tell me, how was your ride with the Horseman? Did you two stop for a bit of sparkin' out under some big oak tree or anything the like?"

"Oh, heavens no!" Briney assured her friend—all the while wishing Gunner had at least tried to kiss her. She blushed at the memory of having been nudged into Gunner's arms by Brown Bonnie, however. "Although, he did embrace me twice today."

"What?" Bethanne exclaimed with excitement. "Do tell, Briney Thress! Do tell!"

Briney giggled with the pleasure of the memory of being held in Gunner's arms. "Well, truth be told, the first time was my fault—because I was so excited in finally owning Sassafras myself that I actually threw my arms around his neck and embraced him with thanks."

"Scandalous!" Bethanne teased with a wink. Briney smiled as Bethanne tugged on the lines a bit, saying, "Slow down, Matilda. Briney and I have a lot to discuss on this short trip home." She smiled at Briney and prodded, "Go on."

"When I realized what I'd done, I was just mortified, of course. I mean, how inappropriate was it for me to hug him like that?" Briney explained.

Bethanne rolled her eyes with exasperation, however. "So that's it? You hugged him?"

"No, not all of it," Briney told her. "When I realized what I was doing, I began to let go of him, only to find that he had wrapped his arms around me…and didn't release me right away. So I stood there, admittedly overwhelmed with bliss, as Gunner Cole just held me in his arms—tight…right up against himself."

"Ooo! How delicious, Briney!" Bethanne giggled.

"Oh, it was delicious! And that wasn't even the end of it," Briney continued. "Then when we were out riding together, we paused and dismounted so that he could show me some of his mares that will be foaling sometime at the beginning of the new year. And as I was turning away from the horses in preparation to leave, one of them nudged me from behind, and I went tumbling forward right into

Gunner's arms, again! And then he caressed my cheek with the back of his hand. And I tell you, Bethanne, I thought I might swoon dead away!"

Bethanne sighed with contentment. "You're gonna end up marryin' the Horseman, Briney. I just know it!"

"Oh, don't be silly, Bethanne," Briney said—although the daydream of marrying Gunner had been in Briney's thoughts from the moment she had first set eyes on him.

"Nope. It's true," Bethanne insisted. "You're gonna marry the Horseman, and I'm gonna marry Charlie Plummer, and we'll both be so happy, you and I. Charlie's going to start raisin' his own horses too, you know. Mr. Cole has already helped him to secure some property nearby so they can work together with the horses." Bethanne tossed her head with joy. "Life is going to be wonderful for us, Briney! Just wonderful!"

Briney shook her head, however, for as much as she wanted to believe what Bethanne was hoping would come true—Briney one day marrying Gunner and Bethanne one day marrying Charlie—it just seemed far too inconceivable that everything would work out to be as perfect as the ending of a storybook.

"You're quiet," Bethanne noted. "It means your doubtin' what I just said. But don't doubt, Briney. Wish and hope and have a little faith. I've already seen it in my mind's eye. We'll both be married and settled down by the end of the year." Bethanne smiled, adding, "Long before the Horseman's mares foal."

"I wish I had your confidence, Bethanne," Briney admitted. "But for pity's sake, I hardly know the man!"

"Oh, I see that sparkle in your eyes, Briney Thress," Bethanne said. "You've been daydreamin' about him since the day you met him, haven't you?"

"Daydreams are only fantasy, Bethanne," Briney answered, avoiding a direct affirmation that Bethanne had hit the nail squarely on the proverbial head. "They don't really come true. Or at least, they rarely do."

But Bethanne's brows suddenly furrowed into a frown as Matilda pulled the buggy into Oakmont.

"What's goin' on, I wonder?" Bethanne asked.

Following Bethanne's gaze, Briney felt a frown furrow her brow as well. A large, ornate carriage was waiting in front of the boardinghouse—rigged to two beautiful black horses. Briney had seen this type of carriage before—in big cities she'd visited with Mrs. Fletcher. This was the conveyance of the wealthy, and a terrible anxiety began to rise in her.

As her mind whispered to her that the carriage in front of the boardinghouse surely had something to do with Mrs. Fletcher herself, and thereby Briney, she began to tremble with trepidation. Yet the sensible part of her thoughts reminded her that Mrs. Fletcher was dead. Therefore, it couldn't be Mrs. Fletcher who had hired the ornate carriage to convey her to Oakmont.

And yet it was in that moment that Mr. Kelley stepped out of the boardinghouse front door, accompanied by a man Briney indeed recognized.

"Mr. Christensen," Briney gasped in horror.

"Who?" Bethanne inquired. She looked to Briney, saying, "Briney! You've gone as pale as a ghost!"

"It's Mr. Christensen…Mrs. Fletcher's solicitor," Briney breathed.

It was as if the joy had been sucked from her somehow. Just the sight of Mr. Christensen had drained Briney Thress of all happiness, all good things, all hopeful dreams and Bethanne's prediction of Briney's marrying Gunner.

"Why would he travel out here?" Bethanne again glanced to Briney. "To see you? Why?"

"I don't know," Briney admitted. "But I've learned from experience that wherever Mr. Christensen goes…misery always follows."

And it was true. Briney remembered the first time she met Mr. Christensen—in a court of law when the legalities of Briney's adoption by Mrs. Fletcher were being finalized. It had been Mr. Christensen who had set down the parameters of Briney's leaving the orphanage to become a ward of Mrs. Fletcher, Mr. Christensen who had drawn up the documents stating that Briney would not be allowed to share the Fletcher family name, that she would have no inheritance of the Fletcher family fortune, that she would be only a ward and companion of Mrs. Fletcher, and that when Mrs. Fletcher no longer had need of Briney's company or service, Briney would then make her own way in the world.

Of course, everything Mr. Christensen had informed the judge of as to Briney's adoptive circumstances had been at Mrs. Fletcher's instruction. Still, Briney resented a man who would bow to such demands where a young girl's life was concerned.

"You've got your own life here, Briney," Bethanne reminded her friend. She pulled Matilda to a halt behind the ornate carriage that had brought Mr. Christensen to town. "That mean old lady is gone! She can't make your decisions for you any more. You're free; remember that. No matter what her solicitor is here to do."

Briney looked to Bethanne, choking back tears of foreboding. "But why is he here?" she asked.

"It doesn't matter, Briney. Not a whit," Bethanne told her. "Let's just march up to him and find out why he's here. He can't hurt you, Briney. Not with that old badger dead and buried."

Briney managed a nod in agreement. Bethanne was right: Mrs. Fletcher couldn't control her life from the grave. Perhaps Mr. Christensen had only arrived to inform her that Mrs. Fletcher was indeed buried and that Briney was free of her forever.

"You're right," Briney said to her friend. "I'll just walk straight up to him and find out his purpose. I well remember the stipulations he announced to the judge upon Mrs. Fletcher's adopting me. I'm free of her…no matter what."

"I'll come with you," Bethanne said, hopping out of the buggy and securing Matilda's lines to the hitching post. "And Daddy's right there too. You have nothin' to fear, Briney. Not with all of us who love you so much at your side."

Briney smiled, brushed a tear from her cheek, and choked in a whisper, "Thank you, Bethanne. Do you know no one has ever actually told me they loved me? Not that I remember, at least."

"Well, I do!" Bethanne stated. "And so do Daddy and Mama…and your handsome Horseman. So have no fear, Briney Thress. Have no fear."

Though Briney knew Gunner Cole didn't love her, she felt he did like her—and Bethanne and her parents had shown her more kindness and love than she'd ever known. Therefore, gathering her courage, Briney stepped down from the buggy as well. And as Bethanne linked arms with her in showing support and care, Briney made her way toward Mr. Christensen.

"Well, here she is now," Mr. Kelley said as Briney and Bethanne approached.

Briney couldn't help but glance into Mr. Christensen's carriage as she passed, and her heart plunged to the very pit of her stomach with anxiety when she saw two women wearing black mourning crape and veils and one man dressed in black still sitting inside the carriage.

"Who are they?" Bethanne asked in a whisper.

"Mrs. Fletcher's children," Briney managed to answer.

All at once, Briney began to tremble as memories of the ill treatment she'd suffered at the hands of Mrs. Fletcher's children began to wash over her like a flood. Always taunting her, referring to her as the ugly orphan duck their mother had saved from the vile orphanage when she was first brought to their home, Nimrod, Mary, and Constance Fletcher had heaped so much misery upon Briney that, try as she might not to, she nearly loathed them.

Certainly, there was the fact that Constance, the youngest of Mrs. Fletcher's children and only two years younger than Briney herself, had eventually changed her inward attitude toward Briney. Eventually, over the past few years, Constance had gotten to where she was almost kind to Briney—but only in private. And though she had ceased in saying hurtful, hateful things to Briney whenever her elder brother and sister were doing so, she did nothing in Briney's defense. Thus, Briney had no fond memories of the Fletcher children—only a desire to never have to see them again. And yet there they were—sitting in a wealthy carriage in what was Briney's haven from them and everything they represented.

"Ah, Briney," Mr. Christensen sternly greeted, "we've been waiting for you near to an hour now."

Briney opened her mouth to apologize, but it was Bethanne who answered, "We've been out ridin' today."

Briney found that Bethanne's defense of her spurred her own courage, and she added, "Yes. I've been riding. And being that you did not send any sort of notification that you were traveling to see me, your wait was no one's fault but yours, Mr. Christensen. I'm no longer subject to your whims." Glancing into the carriage to see the startled expressions on the faces of Mrs. Fletcher's children, Briney's independence strengthened her even more, and she added, "As you should well remember, being that you were the one who drew up the terms of my leaving the orphanage for Mrs. Fletcher's sake."

Mr. Christensen's beady eyes narrowed. His thin lips pursed, and he tugged at his coat lapel. Running cold-looking, boney fingers through his sparse gray hair, he said, "I've come with documents you must sign."

"Documents?" Briney asked, frowning.

"Yes. Documents pertaining to Mrs. Enola Fletcher's will...specifically her estate," he informed her.

"I'm not mentioned in her will, Mr. Christensen," Briney said, "another fact you are well aware of."

Mr. Christensen's lips pursed more tightly—though Briney would have thought it impossible for them to do so.

"Mrs. Fletcher's surviving family—her children, Nimrod, Mary, and Constance—retained me to draw up documents for your signature, stating that you will in no way and never contest any part of Mrs. Fletcher's will, that you will not attempt to lay any legal claim to any part of her estate, which she divided evenly between her three children."

Briney burst into laughter. She couldn't keep from it.

"Are you telling me that those three idiots truly think I would want anything at all to do with any part of Mrs. Fletcher's estate?" she asked him through her astonished amusement. Again she laughed. "You might as well assume I'd want someone to hand me over a souvenir of purgatory!" Again Briney laughed, this time at the sudden and complete feeling of freedom she was experiencing in that moment.

"Oh, do please present your documents to me, Mr. Christensen," she began, "that I may read them, sign them, and send you and Mrs. Fletcher's selfish progeny on your way!"

"Really, Briney," Mr. Christensen said as be began to leaf through the papers in his satchel, "I would've expected more gratitude from you. After all, Mrs. Fletcher did provide you with a lifestyle that most orphan girls would have—"

"Stop! Cease in speaking!" Briney demanded. "Present your papers to me, and do not speak again until I've read them."

"Damn right," Mr. Kelley mumbled, frowning with disgust as he studied Mr. Christensen.

Mr. Christensen did indeed hand a paper to Briney. And as she read it over, she found herself giggling at the nonsense of it all. It was nothing but a bunch of legal jargon stipulating that Briney promised never to contest any part of Mrs. Fletcher's will—never to attempt to gain any property, money, or any other items from Mrs. Fletcher's surviving family.

In truth, as Briney read the document, her heart softened a bit toward Mrs. Fletcher, for the old woman had apparently known her children well—known that they would not feel any obligation to assist Briney financially in carving her own life. It was why Mrs. Fletcher had given Briney all the money in her possession before she'd passed. Briney knew then that as Mrs. Fletcher prepared to meet her Maker, she'd thought of Briney and known she would have no way to live—and that her own children certainly wouldn't help the orphan she'd adopted as her companion. Whether Mrs. Fletcher's intentions had been to face her Maker without any guilt where Briney was concerned or her heart had sincerely been softened toward the girl who had been at her side for ten years, in that moment, Briney was even more thankful that the old woman had secretly gifted her the large sum of money she had before giving up the ghost.

The document was simple and straightforward. In signing it, Briney was legally cutting any and all ties to the Fletchers and their fortune. Thus, Briney plopped down on the front porch of the boardinghouse, intentionally snapping her fingers at Mr. Christensen the way she'd seen Mrs. Fletcher do when she was demanding something of the man—flexing her wealth and position over him. It was not kind, of course, but Briney wanted to see Mr. Christensen and the Fletcher heirs on their way as quickly as possible.

"I assume you have ink and pen," she said to him. "I mean to sign this document here and now and see you on your way."

She glanced up to the carriage as Mr. Christensen began rummaging in his satchel once more in search of ink and pen.

"I suppose you three made this long trip simply to see for yourselves that you had no further fears of ever having to lay eyes on me again, hmmm?" Briney asked—though not in anger. For she truly was feeling free of it all—of wealth, of resentment.

"Yes," Nimrod answered.

"Well, rest assured, Nimrod Fletcher, that I'm as happy to sign this as you are to see me sign it," Briney said—again, not with malice, just a euphoric sense of freedom.

Briney dipped the pen tip into the ink Mr. Christensen had provided. And as she signed her name, she was joyous she was able to sign "Briney Thress" instead of "Briney Fletcher." She'd always been glad Mrs. Fletcher hadn't insisted Briney take her name—for it was all she had left of the parents she'd never known.

"There," she said, blowing breath on the ink to hurry its drying. "For you, Mr. Christensen, with my thanks for bringing it to me."

"Briney?"

Constance's voice startled Briney, as she looked up to see that Constance had left the carriage and was standing over her.

"I…I found this among Mother's things and wanted to give it to you," Constance explained. As she offered a weathered wooden box about the size of a loaf of bread to Briney, she continued, "There's a note inside. It says that these are the things that were brought with you when you entered the orphanage as a baby. They're yours. I'm sorry Mother never gave them to you."

"Constance!" Nimrod growled. "If Mother kept them from her, she had her reasons," he scolded his sister.

Mary placed an arm on Nimrod's shoulder, however, saying, "The box belongs to Briney, brother. You have what you came for. Now leave her be."

"Thank you, Constance," Briney said as she accepted the box. Her heart was hammering with excitement. Yet her joy at knowing there was something from her beginning—perhaps even something of her mother's or father's—was mingled with sadness at the stark realization she would never know them in her earthly life.

Looking up to Constance, Briney reached out and took one of Constance's hands in her own. "Thank you, Constance. Truly. This means so much."

To her astonishment, Constance reached down, throwing her arms around Briney's neck. "We treated you so terribly, Briney! I'm so very sorry!"

Returning Constance's embrace, Briney said, "I wish you only happiness, Constance. And thank you for the box. I will treasure it always and always be thankful that you thought of me enough to see that I received it. Thank you."

Constance brushed tears from her cheeks and hurried back to the carriage.

Mr. Christensen had his pen, ink, and legal document secured in his satchel once more. "That concludes our business then, Briney," he said, offering Briney his hand as she stood.

"Miss Thress," Briney corrected him as she shook his hand politely. To Briney's way of thinking, Mr. Christensen had no right to call her by her first given name. He was no friend or intimate acquaintance.

With pursed lips of aggravation and offense, Mr. Christensen stepped up into the carriage.

"Our business is finished here, Mr. Fletcher," Mr. Christensen pouted.

"Driver!" Nimrod growled.

As the carriage carrying the Fletcher heirs and their solicitor drove away, Briney's heart felt lightened and free of resentment and fear.

"Welcome home for good, my girl!" Mr. Kelley exclaimed, drawing Briney into a tight, loving embrace. He chuckled, adding, "You sure gave that lawyer fella a dose, didn't you?"

"I was too harsh, I'm sure," Briney admitted, feeling somewhat guilty for her terse manner.

"Ah, hell! They deserved it," Mr. Kelley assured her.

Bethanne smiled at Briney, offered an affectionate embrace, and then asked, "What do you suppose is in the box?"

Briney shrugged. "I don't know." Smiling, she added, "How about we find a table in the restaurant, ask your mama if she has any pie left, and see? What do you say?"

"I say, let's!" Bethanne giggled.

❦

That evening, after Briney had finished having supper with the Kelley family, she retired to her room. Although she hoped to hear Gunner's voice outside her window, Mrs. Kelley had mentioned that Gunner had not come to have supper at the restaurant that night.

Although Briney was disappointed that tonight she would have to imagine his voice as she went to sleep instead of actually hearing it, she was glad to have the box Constance had given her. She knew it was something she would cherish, love, and look through for all the days of her life. And with Gunner apparently supping at his own house that night, Briney decided to savor the tender feelings the box's contents evoked in her for the fourth time that same day.

The box was simply made and old. Inside it held very little, but the few items it cached were priceless to Briney.

Sitting on her bed with the box on her lap, Briney opened it, removing what had instantly been her favorite treasure—a silver locket. Carefully she opened the locket, gazing at the two tintype images placed inside it, one on each half of the locket. These were her parents. A note had been left wrapped around the locket, with the words, *Sean and Bindy Thress. Parents of Briney Thress, lost to typhoid fever when Briney was aged 1 year.*

Her mother had been beautiful and her father so very handsome! Upon seeing the images in the locket, Bethanne had remarked that Briney was the very image of her mother—and that knowledge warmed Briney's heart to the core. Now when she looked in the mirror, she knew it was a refection akin to her mother's.

There was a small quilt in the box as well, and Briney could not help but wonder whether her own mother had stitched it for her. It was likely she had. Also in the box was a small toy horse carved from a piece of wood. She wondered whether her father had carved it, and her heart felt that he did.

Other than a note written by an unnamed person—stating that the box and its contents had accompanied the admittance to the orphan asylum of Briney Thress and that the box and its contents should be presented to her upon her dismissal from the institution—that was all the box contained: a locket, a small quilt, and a whittled toy horse.

But to Briney it was more than enough, more than she'd ever had before—a connection to her parents and her true self.

Briney closed the box, placing it carefully in her trunk at the foot of her bed. And though she slipped beneath her blankets disappointed that Gunner's voice wouldn't be lulling her to sleep that night, she was so soothed by a sense of knowing who she was—who her parents had been—that her mind felt at peace in a way it never had before.

She determined that in the morning she would walk out to the Horseman's ranch. She would take the tin of coins with her and bury it deep in one corner of Sassafras's stall. Then she would ride out on her own horse to wherever she and Sassy decided to ride. And if she were lucky—if the fates were being kind—perhaps Gunner would ride out with her again.

Briney smiled as she laid back in her bed and thought of Gunner. Perhaps Bethanne was right. Perhaps Briney could win the heart of the handsome horseman for her own. After all, this one day had gifted things to Briney she never would have dreamed it could have—the longed-for knowledge of her past and her parents, a horse of her own, and a rather shocking measure of affectionate flirtation from the man she had already fallen in love with.

Closing her eyes, she imagined the kind of home she would make for Gunner if she did win him—the kind of home she'd forever longed for herself but never thought she would be blessed to enjoy. A small, cozy home with a warm hearth fire on cool nights, before which she and Gunner would settle to rest after a day of hard work. A home that ever smelled of fresh-baked bread, pies, and warm stew, where the prevailing sounds were the kind and loving words exchanged between parents and children, and the moments of happy laughter the family would share. Beds would be clean and comfortable, with white sheets and quilts Briney herself would stitch. And above all else there would be love.

It was a far-fetched imagining at best. But Briney chose to drift to sleep on the wings of it. If Gunner's voice couldn't carry her to slumber that night, then her hopes and dreams of him would.

"Gunner Cole," Briney whispered to herself. "Gunner and Briney Cole," she softly giggled. "Oh, what heaven would that be?"

CHAPTER SEVEN

It was afternoon when Briney began her walk to Gunner's ranch. She'd spent a wonderful morning with Bethanne and Mrs. Kelley, learning how to make Mrs. Kelley's delicious peach pie. She was proud of her work and had brought a pie with her, intending it for Gunner.

"My mother always told me that the way to a man's heart is through his stomach," Bethanne had said to Briney just before she'd left to walk to the Horseman's ranch to ride Sassafras. "So you take one of those peach pies you baked, and you win Gunner Cole's heart for good!"

At first, Briney had not wanted to take the pie, thinking it would seem rather like a ploy to Gunner—an obvious attempt to win him over.

"So what if it does?" Bethanne had asked. "I'm sure a man wants to know a woman is sweet on him, as much as a woman wants to know a man is sweet on her. So take that pie, Briney."

Thus, Briney found herself on the crest of the hill overlooking Gunner's ranch, holding a peach pie and preparing to see if it were good enough to help her win his heart.

She paused, glancing to the north a moment and frowning when she saw the dark clouds gathering in the distance. She shrugged, however, thinking that getting caught riding Sassafras in the rain surely couldn't be any worse than having her face sunburned to a crisp for having ridden out in the sunshine for too long.

Anyway, it was almost three miles back to town and less than half a mile to Gunner's largest stable. So quickening her step, Briney hurried down the hill toward the ranch.

She was disappointed when she drew near, however, to see Gunner and Charlie exit the big stables accompanied by three men in Cavalry uniforms. Her hopes of Gunner being able to ride out with her were dashed, but at least she had the pie for him. Of course, she worried that offering him the pie with Charlie and three Cavalry men looking on might be too brazen. Still, she didn't want to walk three miles home without at least seeing Gunner. And she did so want to ride Sassafras.

"Afternoon, Briney," Gunner greeted as she approached the group of men. Looking to one of the Cavalry men, obviously an officer, Gunner said, "Pardon me a moment, won't you, Lieutenant? I'll be right back with you."

Striding to meet Briney, Gunner smiled one of his dazzling smiles as he looked at her. "Well, ain't you a nice surprise," he said. "Are you plannin' on takin' Sassy out?"

"Yes," Briney answered. Her heart was racing! "If that's all right with you, of course."

Gunner chuckled. "I told you, she's yours. You can ride her anytime you want. If you give me, oh, half an hour or so, I can help you tack up." His eyes narrowed, and he winked at her. "And if you wouldn't mind, I could ride out with you a ways at least. Unless you would rather ride alone today."

"Oh no!" Briney assured him, feeling almost desperate to have his company while riding. "I would love to have you ride with me. I...I just want to make sure it wouldn't be an imposition." She glanced past him to the waiting Cavalry men still conversing with Charlie.

"Oh, darlin', you could never be an imposition," Gunner said.

Again Gunner's blue eyes seemed to smolder with desire as he continued to stare at Briney. In fact, she was so overwhelmed by the excitement beginning to course through her at being so close to him and under his wildly alluring gaze that she suddenly babbled, "I've brought you a peach pie, as well, as my thanks for helping me with Sassafras and everything. Of course, I baked it, so I'm sure it's not as good as Mrs. Kelley's. But I hope you'll enjoy it all the same."

Taking the pie from her hands, Gunner lifted the dishcloth she'd placed over it and inhaled its fresh, sweet aroma.

"Mmm mmm!" he moaned. "I'm gonna have to hide this away for me and myself only. And I'm sure if you baked it, it's the tastiest pie ever made."

Gunner had been restless all night long. He'd spent the previous night tossing and turning—worrying that if he didn't throw his hat in the ring to claim Briney Thress, one of the other men in town surely would. It wasn't until after he'd decided to pursue the pretty girl that had captured his heart the first day she'd ridden his horse—pursue her with the persistence of a posse chasing an outlaw next time he saw her—that he was able to fall asleep at last.

Gunner had been distracted all morning as he tried to keep up with everything that needed doing at the ranch so he could ride into town for supper at the Kelleys' restaurant as a chance to call on Briney. Gunner's daddy had always told him not to let the grass grow under his feet when he felt strongly about doing something—no matter what it was. And Gunner felt strongly about winning Briney, that was for sure and for certain.

And now here she stood, having walked right up to him—even handed him a pie—and he had to fiddle with the Cavalry boys. Still, he figured he could wrap up his business with them quick enough. After all, they were only giving him the number of horses they wanted, and he simply had to give them a price to get them on their way. They wouldn't be back for near to a fortnight to collect and pay.

"Here," Gunner said, handing the pie back to Briney. "You go on ahead and see Sassy. And put this somewhere safe until I can get away from these fellas, all right? I'll be in shortly to join you." He reached out, caressing the back of her soft cheek with his hand. "I promise it won't take long."

She blushed, biting her lip with delight, and Gunner winked at her once more.

"Of course," she said.

Stepping around him and heading for the barn, Briney called, "Good afternoon, Charlie…gentlemen."

Gunner rubbed his hands together with anticipation of spending the afternoon with Briney. Turning on his heels, he marched back to where Charlie and the others stood, announcing, "All right, boys, let's get this done so we can all get on with what else needs doin'."

Briney entered the stable and was immediately met by all the scents of horses and leather she was fast growing to love more and more. Quickly finding a shelf on which to place the pie, she looked around her, glad to see a shovel close at hand.

Taking the shovel, she hurried to Sassafras's stall. "Hello, sweetheart," she greeted the horse. "You don't mind if I come in for a bit, do you?"

Briney knew Sassy didn't mind, for she'd spent near to an hour learning how to muck out her stall the day before under Gunner's tutelage. Stepping into the horse's domain, Briney quickly closed the stable door behind her to ensure the horse would not leave it.

Then, going to one front corner of the stall and using the shovel to clear the straw away, she hastily dug a hole in the dirt. When she'd dug to a bit over a foot deep, she reached into the pocket of her riding skirt and removed the small jam jar she'd asked Mrs. Kelley for earlier.

Briney had determined that morning that the tins of coins Mrs. Fletcher had given her were simply too heavy to carry unnoticed for three miles, especially when Briney would be carrying a peach pie as well. Therefore, she'd asked Mrs. Kelley if she could purchase a small, empty canning jar for something she was working on. Naturally, Mrs. Kelley had assured Briney that she could simply have the jar; there was no need to pay for it.

And so Briney had packed the jar with as many silver dollars as she could. She figured she could bury a jar every week or so, each containing fifty dollars—the amount of coins necessary to fill Mrs. Kelley's jam jar—and within no time at all, part of her savings would be safely tucked away with her beloved Sassafras.

Once she had buried the jar, she packed the dirt covering her cache and spread the straw over the space before returning the shovel to its proper place.

"Here you are, Sassy," Briney said, giving her horse a large carrot she'd acquired from Mrs. Kelley's kitchen. "There now. Don't you tell anyone our little secret, all right?"

Standing outside of Sassy's stall, she lovingly rubbed the horse's jaw, talking to her as easily as she talked to Bethanne.

"It looks rather cloudy out today, Sassy," she said. "Are you still up for a ride? Even in the rain perhaps?"

The horse whinnied, nodding her head as if she'd actually understood exactly what Briney had told her.

It was only a few more minutes before Gunner came sauntering into the stables. Yet as he did, one of the horses in a front-most stall coughed or sneezed, sending the contents of its nose to splattering on one sleeve of Gunner's shirt.

Stopping in his tracks, Gunner grumbled, "Dammit, Shakespeare! I swear you're doin' that on purpose." Briney's eyes widened as Gunner proceeded to unbutton his shirt and strip it from his body. "You keep that up, boy, and I'll move you to one of the small stables, out back with Stackhouse. Damn horse snot everywhere."

Briney covered her mouth in an effort to stifle her giggle. There was something amusing about seeing a stabled horse get the better of a man like Gunner Cole.

"Boss?" Charlie said, stepping into the stable then. "It looks like it's gonna start comin' down any minute. The Cavalry's moved on, so do you mind if I head over to the bunkhouse to wait it out?"

"That's fine, Charlie, you know that," Gunner said, wadding up his soiled shirt and tossing it into a large wooden box that stood nearby. Charlie turned and jogged away, and Gunner grumbled, "That's three shirts this week, Shakespeare. Dammit to hell!"

All at once, however, Gunner seemed to remember that Briney was watching. Reaching up to rub his whiskery chin, he exhaled a heavy sigh, placed his hands on his hips, and said, "My apologies, Briney," he said. Shaking his head, he continued, "That ain't proper language to use in front of a lady. It's just that Shakespeare here…well, he likes to try and get my dander up, and when I'm in a hurry, I forget to stay clear of him."

Gunner removed his hat, raked his fingers through his hair, and started toward her again. "I hope you don't judge me too harshly on my bad behavior just now."

But Briney couldn't speak, being paralyzed and mute at how entirely provocative—how entirely seductive—Gunner appeared. She'd heard the word *seductive* used in hushed tones throughout her life—knew what it meant. But never before had she owned a true understanding of what it meant; never had she seen anything to exemplify it—until now.

As Gunner stood before her, apologizing once more for his rant because of Shakespeare, she didn't hear a word he was saying, for she was overpowered by his presence—by her unmatched attraction to him.

His muscular torso and arms were bronzed from hours in the sun, his skin as smooth as polished marble. Furthermore, the tousled condition of his chestnut hair—for he still hadn't returned his hat to his head, a gesture of humility and sincere apology—somehow only intensified his good looks. As his strong hands continually turned his hat over and over, the powerful muscles in his forearms were all the more evident.

"Do you forgive me then?" he asked, finally rattling Briney from her admiration of him.

Briney smiled at him. "I'm the one who should apologize…for being amused by Shakespeare's antics."

Gunner rather plopped his hat back onto his head so that it sat low, just above his brow. Then, as the first few drops of rain began to dance on the stable roof, he shrugged his broad shoulders and said, "And now it's rainin', and I can't get back to the house for a clean shirt."

Briney said nothing in response—only continued to smile at him. Though propriety demanded she shouldn't, she liked seeing him in such a state of undress. She liked the way his hat was rather catawampus and that he had to tip his head back a little in order to look at her from under its brim. He was indescribably alluring, and she was glad the rain was starting so that he couldn't get back to the house for a clean shirt.

"It looks like you might be stuck here a while, Briney Thress," he said then, a mischievous grin spreading across his face. "So...you wanna climb up to the hayloft with me and watch the thunderhead roll in?"

Briney felt her own smile broaden. "Oh my, yes!" she assured him with exuberance.

Gunner's grin became a smile, and he reached up, securing his hat to a more comfortable position. "Come on then," he said, holding one hand out to her. "It looks to be a powerful storm. We oughta be able to see the lightnin' strikin' over near town from here."

Placing her hand in his, Briney was instantly awash with bliss from the warm strength of his grip.

"This way, darlin'," Gunner said, winking at her as he headed toward the ladder leading to the front loft of the stable.

Sassafras whinnied, and Gunner looked over his shoulder, saying, "Oh, you be patient. You'll get your turn. You don't like to ride in the rain much anyhow."

"After you," Gunner said, stepping aside so that Briney could climb the ladder up before him.

Briney giggled and began climbing. And as she stepped off the ladder and into the loft, the sweet smell of hay filled her lungs with comfort. She could smell the storm coming as well—smell the easy drops of rain that were falling, moistening the dirt—and she thought that the aroma of rain on the dry soil and grasses of the west was one of the most beautiful she'd ever experienced.

"See there?" Gunner asked, pointing out the open loft doors to the north. "See that big thunderhead out there? It'll be here soon enough and drench us. We sure can use the water too."

Off in the distance, Briney could see the dark, roiling clouds slowly billowing out in every direction. Yet in a mere matter of moments, the thunderhead's boil turned from blue and ominous to a golden warm as it seemed to somehow envelop the sun in its powerful embrace as it rose up.

Briney startled, surprised by the bright strike of lightning that leapt from the clouds, sending thunder to echo off the nearby mountains. It was a sight Briney had never witnessed before, and it was purely awe-inspiring—magnificent in its simple power.

She closed her eyes a moment, deeply inhaling the scents of fresh hay and rain hitting dry dirt and grass. There were no other sounds— just the rain on the roof of the stables and the thunder in the distance.

"I've never seen the like of this," Briney said, opening her eyes to see Gunner staring at her through narrowed, blue smoldering eyes.

"It's beautiful, isn't it?" he asked in a low, syrupy voice that caused a thrilling quiver to travel over her spine. "But not near as beautiful as you are."

Briney blushed. She was delighted by his compliment and flirting but also somewhat scared, for she truly had no experience with men—and she wanted this man more than anything in all her life.

"Flattery isn't necessary, Gunner. I've already promised you I'd leave the peach pie," she teased.

A bold, brilliant lightning strike sent more thunder echoing over the valley. The air was indeed cooler than it had been only minutes before, and Briney rubbed at the chilled goose pimples on her arms.

"You're chilly," Gunner said, reaching out to take Briney's arms in his strong hands. "And here I am with no shirt to offer you for warmth." He winked at her, lowered his voice, and said, "I really ain't much of a gentleman, now am I?"

"I...I th-think you're a very fine gentleman," Briney stammered. "After all, you did notice I was chilled."

She was mesmerized by Gunner's mouth for some reason, her heart leaping in her chest when she saw him slightly moisten his lips.

"Well, I don't know about that," he mumbled, "'cause I don't know if a gentleman would be thinkin' about doin' what I'm thinkin' about doin' right now."

Briney was breathless! She felt her mouth was overly moist and as if her knees were not to be trusted to keep her standing.

"And what's that?" she managed to ask in a whisper.

Gunner released her a moment, taking his hat from his head and tossing it to the pile of hay nearby.

"Oh, I'm thinkin'," he began, taking her waist between his hands and pulling her closer to him, "I'm thinkin' I'm gonna kiss you."

Briney gasped with elation.

"And I'm thinkin' that I ain't even gonna ask your permission," he added, pulling her tight against his body. "What do you say to that, Miss Briney Thress?"

Briney had never been kissed. She'd never known one boy or man long enough to want to be kissed by him—never been alone long enough with a man for him to try to steal a kiss even if she hadn't wanted to kiss him. But the one thing she knew—even without any experience—was that she wanted, more than anything she'd ever wanted, for Gunner to kiss her.

"Hmm," Gunner breathed when Briney didn't answer him. "I'll take that as you ain't against the idea, all right?"

Briney was trembling like a newborn foal! He could feel it in her—the nervous anxiety, the fear, and yet the desire. She wanted him to kiss her; Gunner knew she did. And because he owned a knowledge of her past and guessed at the lack of experience it would've afforded her in dealing with men, he knew he must be careful with her, gentle, especially at first, lest he traumatize her somehow with the power of the passion he was feeling for her—and send her running from his arms forever.

"There ain't a whole lot to it, you know?" he said in a low, calming voice. "Instinct is all you need, darlin'."

Gunner felt Briney's body tense as he cupped her chin in one hand. "You ain't afraid of me, are you? You know you can trust me, Briney. You know you can. You can trust me," he whispered as he pressed his lips lightly to hers.

He felt her knees begin to buckle and was pleased, for it was an indication she was not averse to him.

Taking her arms, he placed them around his own neck. Then wrapping her in his arms and holding her firmly against his body to help support her weight, he kissed her again, this time allowing his lips to linger against hers, until he felt her faint, tentative response—until he felt her kiss him in return.

He felt her surrender to him then—felt her body relax against his—felt her trust—and he kissed her a third time, pressing his lips to hers and coaxing hers to part in meeting his. Sensing that her knees were no longer threatening to give way beneath her, he paused, caressing her cheeks with the backs of his hands.

"I ain't a rounder, you know," he told her. "I don't go lurin' beautiful women up to my hayloft so I can spark with them just for the entertainment's sake. You know that, right?"

Briney nodded at him, and Gunner felt his breath catch in his throat. For what he saw in Briney's eyes as she gazed at him, it was more than trust, more than desire—it was love! The girl loved him already! No matter how implausible it should seem, he could see that she did.

The evidence of Briney's love for him, so marked in her beautiful blue eyes, was his undoing somehow, and Gunner found that he could not keep from claiming her kiss the way he'd dreamt of doing from the moment he first saw her.

Gunner reached out, cradling Briney's face in his hands. She felt the warm caress of his thumb move across the tenderness of her lower lip. And then, all at once, he pulled her into a powerful, very possessive embrace—an embrace she wished she could linger in forever! Instantly, Gunner's mouth captured hers, claimed hers—his mouth, not merely his lips. And Briney's heart threatened to leap from her chest with irrepressible rapture!

Briney could feel the heat of Gunner's skin penetrating her shirtwaist—even her camisole and corset—until her own flesh felt warmed by it. The sense of his smooth skin beneath her palms—the rugged contours of his chest where her hands rested—served to send her into an almost frenzy of desire!

His mouth was hot and moist, tinged with a flavor she could only determine was unique to him—a unique ambrosial taste that created a mad sort of thirst in her she feared could never be quenched.

A loud clap of thunder struck, startling Briney so that she gasped, breaking the seal of their kiss. But Gunner was undaunted by such things as the power of nature and immediately drew her tight against him, raining such an exhilaration over her as his mouth worked to savor hers that Briney vowed never to give him up—never to be parted from him—not for one moment for all the rest of her life.

As the gently falling rain turned to deluge, Briney was no longer aware of the brilliant flashes of lightning or the crashing of thunder as the storm overtook the ranch. To her, there was only Gunner. She gasped when he unexpectedly swept her up into the cradle of his arms, carrying her to a large mound of hay and gently tossing her into it before lying down next to her.

"You're gonna marry me, you know," he told her, grinning as he propped his head up on one hand and studied her a moment. "If I have to tie you up and keep you up here until you agree to it…you will marry me, Briney Thress."

"You don't even know me, Gunner," she reminded him, even as tears of joy trickled from the corner of her eyes.

"Yes, I do," he said. "I knew you the minute I walked into this stable less than a week ago. I knew then I wanted you…that I was already in love with you."

He wiped a tear from her cheek with his thumb. "I know you felt the same, that first day we met. I can see it in your eyes now. You love me too, don't you?"

"I loved you before I even met you, Gunner," she whispered. "I heard your voice most nights after I took to my own room at the boardinghouse. My room is just over the Kelleys' restaurant, and I could hear your voice when you were talking with others in town. Your voice—it's what made me feel safe when Mrs. Fletcher lay dying. Your voice is what made me hope that all would be well."

"Briney! Briney Thress!"

Gunner frowned, quickly standing. "Who's there?" he called.

But Briney recognized the voice already. It was Nimrod Fletcher shouting for her.

"It's Nimrod," she breathed with disappointment. "He probably has some other ridiculous paper he wants me to sign." Briney grumbled.

"Who's Nimrod Fletcher?" Gunner asked.

"Mrs. Fletcher's son," she quickly explained as she rose to her feet and headed for the ladder leading down from the loft. "His solicitor, Mr. Christensen, came to Oakmont yesterday. Nimrod and his sisters accompanied him to ensure that I signed a legal document promising never to contest Mrs. Fletcher's will."

Briney was furious! She'd signed the document demanding she never seek anything at all from the Fletcher heirs. Yet there was Nimrod, shouting as he ever did—shouting up from the stables at her and spoiling the most wonderful moment of her entire life.

"Briney, wait," Gunner said as Briney began to descend the ladder before him.

"He probably just wants to threaten me in some other such way, or call me an ugly orphan duck. How dare he intrude like this! And who does he think he is to come marching onto your property—"

Briney felt the tug at the bottom of her skirt—felt herself slip from the ladder rungs and fall flat on her back onto the stable floor.

The fall knocked the breath from her, and she could only stare up into the enraged expression of Nimrod Fletcher.

CHAPTER EIGHT

"What was in that box Constance gave to you yesterday?" Nimrod growled. "Money? A property deed? Jewels? Whatever it was she gifted you, it does not belong to you! It belongs to we Fletchers!"

Briney couldn't draw breath, and the sensation was terrifying! She couldn't move to defend herself. She was at Nimrod's mercy!

"You signed a legal document forfeiting any claim on anything!" Nimrod raged. "Promising never to contest—"

But Nimrod's furious rant was cut short when Gunner leapt from the loft, knocking Nimrod to the floor next to Briney.

"And who the hell are you?" Gunner roared. Reaching down and taking hold of Nimrod's collar, Gunner pulled the man to his feet. Without another word, Gunner let go a devastating fist to Nimrod's jaw, knocking him to the stable floor once more. "You don't touch Briney! Do you hear me? And you don't walk into my stable and—"

Briney's breath returned only an instant before the gunshot split the air. "Gunner!" Briney screamed as she saw Gunner's hand go to his right shoulder—saw the blood beginning to trickle from the wound.

"Why, you filthy, yellow—" Gunner growled as he moved forward toward Nimrod.

Another shot rang out, and Briney saw blood begin to soak Gunner's blue jeans at his right thigh.

"Stop! Nimrod! Stop!" she cried, pulling at Nimrod's arm in an attempt to capture the pistol he held in his hand.

But Nimrod was mad with rage, and he pointed the pistol at Briney, growling, "What was in the box? Tell me!"

"I won't tell you, not while you've got that gun!" she cried. "Put it down, and I'll tell you! Put it down if you want to know what Constance gave to me!"

Nimrod began to lower the gun, but Gunner rushed him, and another shot rang out!

"No!" Briney screamed, scrambling to her feet. Without pausing to see who had been shot, Briney ran to Sassafras's stall, and flung the door open. Quickly climbing the stall door, Briney took hold of Sassafras's mane, mounting her bareback, forgoing a bridle altogether and taking time only to pull a loose lead rope around her neck.

"If you want what's in the box, you'll have to catch me, Nimrod! You'll have to catch me!" she screamed as she rode Sassafras from the stables at a full gallop.

Crying, sobbing with fear for Gunner's life, Briney rode away from the stable, praying aloud, "Oh, God! Let him follow me and leave Gunner alone! Please, God! Save my love! He is my life now!"

The rain was torrential, and Briney could only trust that Sassafras knew where she was going. And then, over the sound of the rain pummeling the ground, came another noise—a rhythmic pounding. Briney glanced back to see Nimrod astride a massive black stallion and riding after her as if the devil himself had escaped hell to pursue her.

Briney knew Sassafras could never outrun the stallion, and so she reined in—leapt from Sassafras's back and turned to face Nimrod.

Nimrod reined in before her, his face red with rage.

"Do you want to know what was in the box, Nimrod Fletcher?" she shouted to him. She was drenched, cold, and still jarred from her fall from the ladder.

"I do," Nimrod said, leveling his pistol at her.

"One silver dollar, Nimrod," Briney cried out over the rain. "One dollar—that was all Constance gave me."

Briney wanted to know. She wanted to know if Nimrod Fletcher were truly as greedy as he appeared to be—so greedy and heartless that even the thought of Constance's giving Briney one dollar would keep him enraged.

"One dollar that belongs to me!" Nimrod shouted.

"You would kill me over one dollar?" Briney yelled.

"It's my dollar!" Nimrod growled, cocking his pistol.

Briney gasped then as something seemed to jerk Nimrod from his horse. And then a bolt of lightning struck nearby, illuminating the dark of the storm, and Briney saw him—Gunner! He was astride Shakespeare, holding one end of a rope in his hand as Nimrod struggled against the other end at his throat.

Even still, Nimrod once more leveled his pistol at Briney. But the Horseman was not called the Horseman for any trivial purpose. Quickly tossing another lasso, Gunner easily looped Nimrod's hand that held the gun.

"You'll hang for this, you son of a—" Briney heard Gunner shout as he turned Shakespeare and rode hell-bent in the opposite direction, Nimrod Fletcher trailing the ground behind him.

Briney could only watch and sob with being overwrought with relief that Gunner was alive. She felt Sassafras come to stand near her—and both she and Sassy watched as Gunner leapt from Shakespeare's back and began to beat Nimrod with his bare hands.

It was not long before Nimrod's unconscious body lay still in the grass, the rain pouring over him.

Sobbing, Briney raced to Gunner, flinging herself against him and nearly collapsing with relief when she felt the strength of his arms enfold her.

"Are you all right, darlin'?" Gunner asked, taking Briney's face in his hands, gazing into her eyes with concern. "Are you all right? Did he hurt you?" he asked. Without giving her a chance to answer, Gunner's warm mouth met hers—melded with hers in a desperate kiss of reassurance and love.

"I would die if anythin' ever happened to you, Briney," he said. "I *would* die!"

He kissed her again, long and hard, and Briney knew her thirst of his kiss would never be quenched.

"Marry me, Briney," Gunner said over the hammer of the rain. "Marry me tomorrow so I'll never have to spend another night or day without you. Will you marry me tomorrow, Briney Thress?"

"Yes!" Briney cried. "Yes! Oh yes! I love you, Gunner! More than life itself."

"Boss! Boss!" Charlie called, reining in his horse before them. "I heard gunshots, boss! Are you all right?" Charlie looked at Nimrod as he moaned. "And who the hell is that?"

Gunner smiled at Briney, kissed her again, and answered, "Some Nimrod feller. Wanna help me tie him up and haul him to the sheriff in town?"

"Sure thing, boss," Charlie said without another question as he dismounted.

Taking Briney's face in his hands again, Gunner smiled and said, "I guess I better check in with old Doc Chesterfield and get stitched up a bit—bein' as I'm gettin' married tomorrow."

He brushed the tears from Briney's cheeks with his thumbs and then pulled her into his arms, kissing the top of her head.

"What's that, boss?" Charlie called as he kicked Nimrod in one leg until the villain moved.

"I'm gettin' married tomorrow, Charlie," Gunner hollered. Looking back to Briney, he repeated, "I'm gettin' married tomorrow."

"And you don't mind what people in town will think?" Briney asked, kissing him softly on the lips.

"You mean because I ain't known you a whole week yet?" he asked, kissing her in return.

"Because you'll be marrying an orphan," Briney teased.

"Well, you'll be marryin' the grandson of a Quaker man and a harlot," Gunner offered.

"What a pair we'll make then, hmmm?" Briney asked.

"What a pair indeed," Gunner mumbled against Briney's mouth.

"Boss, you want me to haul this guy onto his own horse or what?" Charlie called.

But he received no response—for Briney Thress was in the arms of the man she loved, kissing him with such shared passion that even if the rain hadn't been falling as heavy as any waterfall there ever had been, neither Briney nor Gunner would've been aware of anything in all the world beyond one another.

EPILOGUE

The fire burned warm in the bedroom hearth. The comforting pop and crackle of the cedar burning there filled the room with a sense of languid tranquility. Lightning struck somewhere in the distance, and the soft rumble of the thunder over the valley was to Briney as the soothing sound of a father's voice to his sleepy child.

Setting her stitching aside, Briney Cole gazed at the sight before her on the woolen rug before the fire. There, stretched out in his stockinged feet, lay Gunner—little Adelaide sleeping peacefully on his chest. It was hard to believe her baby was already four months old, and Briney shook her head in the wonder of how quickly time seemed to pass.

Another flash of lightning stirred Gunner from his dozing, and he rubbed his baby's back lovingly before gently moving her from his chest and onto the warm woolen rug. Briney smiled, touched and amused when Gunner stripped off his shirt, using it to cover his sleeping daughter.

Rising to his feet, he strode the few steps to Briney, pulling her from her seat and into his arms.

"What are you grinnin' about, darlin'?" he whispered.

"Just you," she whispered in return.

"Why? Because Adelaide has me wrapped around her little finger just the way you do?" he said, smiling.

"Maybe so," Briney giggled. "But most of all because I just can't believe that I managed to capture the Horseman's attention…let alone his heart."

"The Horseman," Gunner said, shaking his head. "It sounds ridiculous if you ask me."

"No, it doesn't," Briney insisted, "for you are the Horseman— the greatest horseman in all the west."

Gunner smiled, pressed a kiss to Briney's lips, and exhaled a contented sigh. "I'm glad you think so, darlin'."

"I know so," she corrected him.

Kissing her again, Gunner inhaled deeply the scent of her cheek—then of her hair. It was something he'd begun to do every time he held her, beginning on their wedding night—to inhale what he called "the Briney perfume."

"Oh, quit sniffing me, Gunner!" Briney giggled. "I smell like supper."

A low, provocative laugh rumbled in his throat. "You smell like apple pie, my girl," he teased. "And is that pie near to being cooled enough to eat or not? I've been waitin' on it for hours."

"Yes, it's cooled, you silly man," Briney assured him. Placing her arms around his neck and gazing into the beautiful blue smolder of his eyes, she said, "I remember when you found me much more interesting than my pies, Mr. Cole."

Gunner grinned. "Oh, you mean before me and Adelaide fell asleep in front of the fire just now?" he teased.

Briney kissed Gunner on the mouth and then turned, intent on fetching a piece of pie for him. But he caught her by the waist, pulling her back against him.

Placing a lingering kiss on her neck, he asked, "And where do you think you're goin', horsewoman?"

"To get your pie, horseman," she said.

Gunner kissed her neck again, tugging on the neckline of her nightgown until it slipped down over her shoulder and then kissed her shoulder.

It began to rain then—a gentle rain that seemed somehow to tickle the rooftop of the house—and it made Briney smile. Rain always reminded her of the first time Gunner had kissed her, in the loft of the big stable. Her life had changed forever in that moment. In many ways, her life began in that moment. And every time the rain would come, the memory of how wonderful it had been to discover that Gunner Cole—the Horseman—loved her as she loved him.

"You know," Gunner said, kissing her shoulder once more. "Adelaide is sound asleep. As sound asleep as I've ever seen her."

Briney smiled and teased, "Oh good! Then we can eat our pie together and not feel badly that she can't have any yet."

Briney gasped with delight when Gunner suddenly swooped her up into the cradle of his arms.

"Woman, why are you goin' on about pie when you've got the Horseman as your lover, hmmm?" Gunner asked as he carried Briney to their bed. Laying her down upon it and covering her body with his own, he pressed his face to her throat and inhaled deeply. "It's the perfume of heaven to me, you know? The scent of you."

Gunner placed a firm, moist kiss to the hollow of Briney's throat. "I love you so much, Briney," he mumbled against her neck. "I don't know how I ever lived without you before that day you walked in and won over Sassafras."

Briney felt tears welling in her eyes. "Remember, my love, that I loved you first...before we'd even met. That voice of yours! Oh, how I longed to hear it, looked forward to it each evening. Even now, just the sound of your voice makes my heart flutter. I loved you even before that day. I just didn't know it was you I loved."

"So you like my voice, do you, ma'am?" Gunner whispered against her ear.

As goose pimples enveloped Briney's body, she giggled with delight. "Yes, Mr. Horseman, I do."

Trailing lingering, moist kissed from her chin, down her neck, and over her shoulder, Gunner continued. "Then prove it," he mumbled against her mouth.

Wrapping her arms around his neck, Briney kissed Gunner. And it was the kiss of not only impassioned desire but also the promise of an unending love that would endure far beyond mere mortal life.

"I'm your wife," Briney breathed as Gunner tugged the ribbon from her hair. "I still can't believe it sometimes."

Gunner grinned at her, brushed a strand of hair from her forehead, and teasingly asked, "That baby asleep there on the rug ain't evidence enough for you, woman?"

Briney winked at Gunner and said, "I just may need a little more confirmation tonight, that's all."

"Oh, believe me, darlin'...I'm gonna give you some confirmation," Gunner promised.

And as the baby slept warm and safe before the fire—as the rain played a quiet melody upon the rooftop—Briney knew there was nothing more perfect in all the world than having the love of her husband and daughter, all of them safe and warm in their home. It was all she had ever hoped for—dreamt of. It was real, and it existed because of the Horseman.

AUTHOR'S NOTE

The fact of the matter is that I'm a homebody. I like to be home. Home is my haven—the one place in all the world I most like to be. I don't like to travel very much; it stresses me out in a way few people understand, I think. I like my bed, my pillow, my apples, cinnamon, and nutmeg simmering on the stove, my *A Charlie Brown Christmas* music softly wafting through the kitchen and family room. I like to watch my grandchildren play on the family room floor, laugh and laugh and laugh with my husband, children, in-law children, and very close friends—all inside my home. I like to sit at the kitchen table after a meal and just bathe in conversation with loved ones (I think I miss my grandparents most in those moments)—or play a rousing game of cards and whoop and holler, be silly, sing along to my favorite '80s tunes at the top of my lungs with my daughter, sister, or friends. I like to put little tealight candles in the crackle-glass votives on my mantel, sit on my couch, and drink a not too hot, but hot enough, mug of Stephen's Gourmet Candy Cane flavored hot cocoa, and watch my favorite cop shows, holiday movies, or documentaries. I like to bind my quilts by hand while sitting on the same couch and watching the same cop shows, holiday movies, or documentaries. I love to bake and think back to when my mother used to bake and fill our home with warm, sweet smells and tell us we could have as much cake as we wanted. I like to lie in my bed at night and read a children's book or two—books with beautiful illustrations and perfect phrases that relax my mind and help me to settle down and go to sleep. I love to lie in my bed and listen to the wind chimes and crickets, the coyote calls far in the distance, and feel the cool breeze on my arms and face. I just love my home— especially when it's quiet and serene and I can think above the noise of life and take a break from the sometimes-insurmountable stress of it.

Recently I was explaining my lack of desire to travel to a couple of close friends of mine. I had been receiving some insistent pressure to "take a vacation" and was kind of feeling like a loser for not wanting to take a vacation. In fact, I had recently been introduced to the term "staycation"—when one stays home and just takes a vacation from certain responsibilities or social obligations. Wow! Talk about an epiphany! "STAYcation? Eureka!" But I digress. I was explaining to a couple of friends my lack of desire to travel and was so encouraged to hear that neither of them liked to travel either! They both expressed their desire to just stay home and relax. One friend even said, "To me, the best part of a vacation is getting home!" Well put, I say!

Now, I'm not in any way criticizing those who enjoy vacation and travel. More power to you! In truth, I wish I were a bit more amiable to it, but I'm not, and that's just one of my character flaws—or strengths, depending on how you look at it. My point is simply this: Briney's desire for a home, her relief at not having to spend the rest of her entire life traveling the way she had been forced to do during her tenure with Mrs. Fletcher—well, yep, she gets that from me!

As I was thinking over Briney's life as an orphan and then as Mrs. Fletcher's companion, I just knew she had been miserable about never having a home. I also knew that the kind of home she wanted was a home she would never have to leave—one that was so wonderful and filled with love that she wanted to protect it, linger in it, and savor the atmosphere of it, the way I do mine.

So to put it simply, herein lies so much of the inspiration for the bits and pieces that make up the heart of this story. I love to be home, and so does Briney.

Yours,
Marcia Lynn McClure

(And now it's time for "A Few of Marcia's Trivial Snippets!")

Snippet #1—The Pray-to-Plummer Pass Play. As my friend Gina would say, "So…here's the thing." My mom graduated in 1955 from Cañon City High School in Colorado, and among the many stories I remember her telling while I was growing up was the exciting story of Cañon City High's football team and the Pray-to-Plummer pass play. I can still see the twinkle that would leap to her warm brown eyes as she'd recount the exciting football play between the lineman Charles Plummer and end Buster Pray. Apparently, this play was something wonderful and exciting to behold and led to touchdowns, fans cheering with elation, and so on. The Pray-to-Plummer pass play was the stuff of legends—at least in Cañon City—as well as a pretty fun tongue twister for me to grow up repeating to myself. Therefore (and I'm sure you figured this out long ago), since my mom is always,

always on my mind and in my heart and since her memory is failing so quickly and I feel a near desperation to preserve every memory of hers that I am able, Gunner's friend and Bethanne's love interest, Charlie Plummer, is named after Charles "Lanky" Plummer, the 1952 senior class hero of Cañon City High's football team! Also, the stallion that sired Brown Bonnie, Buster Pray, is named after Buster "Bus" Pray, Plummer's counterpart in the Pray-to-Plummer pass play. And all because my mom's voice was echoing "the Pray-to-Plummer pass play" through my memory the day I was inspired to write and introduce Charlie's character. For weeks I wasn't able to get "the Pray-to-Plummer pass play" out of my head. I'm so weird! (Seriously, say it five times fast: The Pray-to-Plummer pass play, the Pray-to-Plummer pass play, the pray-to-prummer prass play. See? It's tougher than you might think!)

Snippet #1 Addendum—FYI, Joe Cotton was a real racehorse. He won the Kentucky Derby in 1885. If you seem to recognize his name, it's because Joe Cotton was the racehorse mentioned in my book *The Windswept Flame*—the horse Cedar Dale was lucky enough to witness win the Derby in 1885. Joe Cotton was rumored to have been killed in an accident in 1888, but in truth Joe was purchased by a man who used him as a breeding stallion. And then between 1895, ten years after winning the Kentucky Derby, Joe Cotton was employed pulling a hack (basically a horse-drawn school bus) and frequently seen until sometime before 1905. As for Old Billy, he was a foundation sire for the American Quarter Horse breed, foaled in 1862. Gunner's stud, Stackhouse, and his mare Brown Bonnie, however—well, Stackhouse is named for the place from whence I order my raspberry almonds every holiday season, and Brown Bonnie just sounded like a cute name. Ha ha!

Snippet #2—How did Sassy the horse get her name? I'm not even sure I should tell you this, but one night while watching one of my documentaries (I *love* documentaries), I learned that one of the notable reasons that the "Old World" countries wanted so desperately to colonize the "New World" was because of the sassafras plant. Sassafras (which grew in abundance in Virginia—i.e., Roanoke and Jamestown) was thought to be just about the only cure for syphilis (which was running rampant in the Old World) at the time. It's kind of gross to think that the British, Spaniards, and French had to colonize a whole new continent because of syphilis! Eww! Of course, that's not the only reason for the colonization, but apparently it was a big one. Nevertheless, as I was watching this documentary on syphilis and sassafras, I made a conscious decision to focus on why sassafras was important in my own life—why, root beer, of course! Root beer—the only soda pop I like, the soda pop of my childhood (my aunt Sharon made dee-double-licious root beer)! Not to mention root bear barrels, the hard candy that tastes like root beer. So as I was sitting watching a documentary on syphilis and sassafras and trying to focus on root beer and sassafras instead, I thought, "Hmmm. Sassafras...that's a good name for a horse."

Snippet #3—Victorian Mourning Dress Rituals. After you read the following, no further explanation will be needed as to why I "relaxed" (well, did away with, in truth) the mourning dress rituals Briney would've been expected to adhere to upon Mrs. Fletcher's death—especially since I wanted Briney's new life of freedom to be bright and happy. Keep in mind that things were somewhat more relaxed here in the western United States. Even so, it was not until World War I that the stringent mourning expectations of the

Victorian era began to change. The Great War necessitated the end of such lengthy (and often expensive) dressing rituals when it came to mourning, simply because so many lives were being lost, and a country shrouded in black would've been a hopeless one indeed.

This is an excerpt from *Polite Society at Home and Abroad*, published in 1891, which is "not in copyright."

A widow's bonnet should be of heavy crape, with white crape or tarlatan border, and the veil must be worn over the face. At the end of three months, she may wear the veil descending from the back of her bonnet. This deep veil must be worn a year, and mourning must be worn two years. Many widows never return to gay colors, and some wear mourning the rest of their lives.

A widower wears mourning for a year. His mourning must consist of a black suit, black gloves and necktie, and a deep weed on his hat. Those who are very punctilious in such matters wear black-edged linen and black studs and cuff-buttons.

For parents or children deep mourning is worn for a year. After that, though mourning is worn another year, the material is changed, and crape is dispensed with.

A sudden transition at the end of the period of mourning, from black to glaring colors, should not be made. Any change of this nature should be gradual.

Crape and soft woolen goods for brothers and sisters are worn for six months; after that gray, black, and white can be adopted.

Of course there are no set limits to the period of wearing mourning, for these matters vary with the individual tastes and feelings of the wearer. Custom has laid down certain rules, which, however, can be widely departed from at will.

For uncles, aunts, cousins, and grandparents, black suits without crape are worn.

Children wear mourning for a parent one year. It seems an unnatural custom to put very small children into deep black, even for so near a friend as a parent. The little ones do not comprehend the loss that has come to them; why teach them the meaning of their sad garb?

Gentlemen in mourning wear weeds, whose depth is proportioned to the closeness of their relationship to the dead. Their mourning is adhered to only as long as the ladies of their household wear it.

(Holy smokes, right?)

Snippet #4—Eugene's Quaker Grandfather. Our family stands in admiration of and with unconditional love for a wonderful couple who are, oh, twenty or so years older than Kevin and I. We find that both Eugene and his wife, Clara, are profoundly wise people. Clara is a true mentor to me—one from whom I've learned more in the few years I've known her than I did from tens of hundreds of people I knew in all those years before. She's my mentor, my friend, my gun buddy, and one of the greatest joys to my heart and soul. As for her husband, Eugene—he's her counterpart, especially to my two sons. Eugene is an incredibly masculine man who has inspired my sons to reach for greatness, as well as to pursue their dreams of working in law enforcement. Yet one of my favorite things about Eugene is— well, he has *awesome* stories! I could go on for hours about some of my favorites, but the one that he gave me permission to tell you is this: Eugene comes from good, righteous Quaker stock. I think this heritage is strong in Eugene, in that I don't know if I've ever heard him speak badly of anyone (politicians not included—but they dig their own graves, if you know what I mean). Continuing on, Eugene's paternal grandfather and grandmother were Quakers. And as the scandalous story goes, after a few children were born to Eugene's Quaker grandparents—well, let me put it simply. Eugene's Quaker grandmother was quite a strict woman…in every aspect of her life—*every* aspect. Thus, you can imagine the utter astonishment (and ensuing scandal) when Eugene's grandfather up and divorced his Quaker wife and married the woman who ran the town brothel! Of course, the story is much more interesting (and detailed) when Eugene is telling it. But it did lend me the inspiration for Gunner's grandparents' colorful past. Eugene's story also inspired me along the paths of Gunner expressing his feelings over not judging people by their heritage or their past but by the person they become. Eugene explained that although he loved his Quaker grandmother, he has much fonder memories of his ex-madam grandmother. To sort of paraphrase a quote from Eugene, "You know, if you were horsing around and broke one of her teacups, she didn't get mad at you." Grandmothers who don't scold their grandchildren for accidentally breaking things are the kind of grandmothers children should have, you know? Oh, that Eugene! He sure has some great stories!

Snippet #5—What's with the peach pie *again*? Okay, I know that peach pie has made an appearance in several of my books—well, at least one that I can think of right offhand (*The Touch of Sage*). And if you're wondering why it was included in this book as well, I'll tell you that I wondered the same thing! I kept thinking, "What's with me and peach pie?" Therefore, I sat down for a moment during this author's note and thought about exactly why peach pie has shown up in another story. And you know what I realized? It's because *I* feel deprived of peach pie! I *love* peach pie, and I never get to have it! Probably because (1) I don't bake nearly as much as I used to— hardly at all in fact. (2) I like *good* peach pie, not so-so peach pie. (3) Peach pie is an essential part of life, and I'm missing out. But fear not! I've made a goal to run down to the Flying Star restaurant in Corrales next week and pick up a piece of peach pie for myself. That way maybe you can imagine the yumminess of some other delicious treat in my next book for a change, okay? (I especially love peach pie when it's warm from the oven, with butter and granulated sugar slathered all over the top crust and with a scoop of high-quality vanilla ice cream on the side! Yikes! I've gotta get out more!)

Snippet #6—Nimrod. As you know, the most famous man named Nimrod was a great hunter, as well as the being the great-grandson of Noah. Thus, originally when someone was referred to as "Nimrod," it referred to his being a hunter. Eventually it became a term among hunters to refer to someone who was a clumsy hunter. So, naturally, Bugs Bunny frequently referred to Elmer Fudd as "Nimrod." The problem was that most people didn't understand the "clumsy hunter" meaning. Therefore, by the early 1980s, "nimrod" had become a synonym for "idiot." So, yes, I did name Nimrod Fletcher because he was an idiot. I guess I am a little too transparent sometimes, hmmm.

Snippet #7—Lastly, if you're wondering why there seem to be some loose ends with this story (such as, "Did Bethanne and Charlie get married?" and "What happened to Nimrod? Did he hang for trying to kill Gunner?"), the answer is this: I simply wanted Gunner and Briney's story to funnel to a focus on just *them*. I wanted us all to feel the way they felt there in the hayloft—how they felt at the end of the book when savoring the warmth and loving atmosphere of their home and family—as if there were no one else in all the world.

My everlasting admiration, gratitude and love…
To my husband, Kevin…
My inspiration…
My heart's desire…
The man of my every dream!

ABOUT THE AUTHOR

Marcia Lynn McClure's intoxicating succession of novels, novellas, and e-books—including *A Crimson Frost, The Visions of Ransom Lake, Kissing Cousins* and *Untethered*—has established her as one of the most favored and engaging authors of true romance. Her unprecedented forte in weaving captivating stories of western, medieval, regency, and contemporary amour void of brusque intimacy has earned her the title "The Queen of Kissing."

Marcia, who was born in Albuquerque, New Mexico, has spent her life intrigued with people, history, love, and romance. A wife, mother, grandmother, family historian, poet, and author, Marcia Lynn McClure spins her tales of splendor for the sake of offering respite through the beauty, mirth, and delight of a worthwhile and wonderful story.

BIBLIOGRAPHY

A Bargained-For Bride

Beneath the Honeysuckle Vine

A Better Reason to Fall in Love

The Bewitching of Amoretta Ipswich

Born for Thorton's Sake

The Chimney Sweep Charm

Christmas Kisses-Three Favorite Holiday Romances

A Crimson Frost

Daydreams

Desert Fire

Divine Deception

Dusty Britches

The Fragrance of her Name

A Good-Lookin' Man

The Haunting of Autumn Lake

The Heavenly Surrender

The Highwayman of Tanglewood

Kiss in the Dark

Kissing Cousins

The Light of the Lovers' Moon

Love Me

The Man of Her Dreams

The McCall Trilogy

Midnight Masquerade

The Object of His Affection

An Old-Fashioned Romance

One Classic Latin Lover, Please

The Pirate Ruse

The Prairie Prince
The Rogue Knight
Romance at the Christmas Tree Lot
The Romancing of Evangeline Ipswich
Romantic Vignettes-The Anthology of Premiere Novellas
Saphyre Snow
Shackles of Honor
The Secret Bliss of Calliope Ipswich
Sudden Storms
Sweet Cherry Ray
Take a Walk with Me
The Tide of the Mermaid Tears
The Time of Aspen Falls
To Echo the Past
The Touch of Sage
The Trove of the Passion Room
Untethered
The Visions of Ransom Lake
Weathered Too Young
The Whispered Kiss
With a Dreamboat in a Hammock
The Windswept Flame

CPSIA information can be obtained at www.ICGtesting.com
Printed in the USA
LVOW10s1105060416

482416LV00002B/314/P